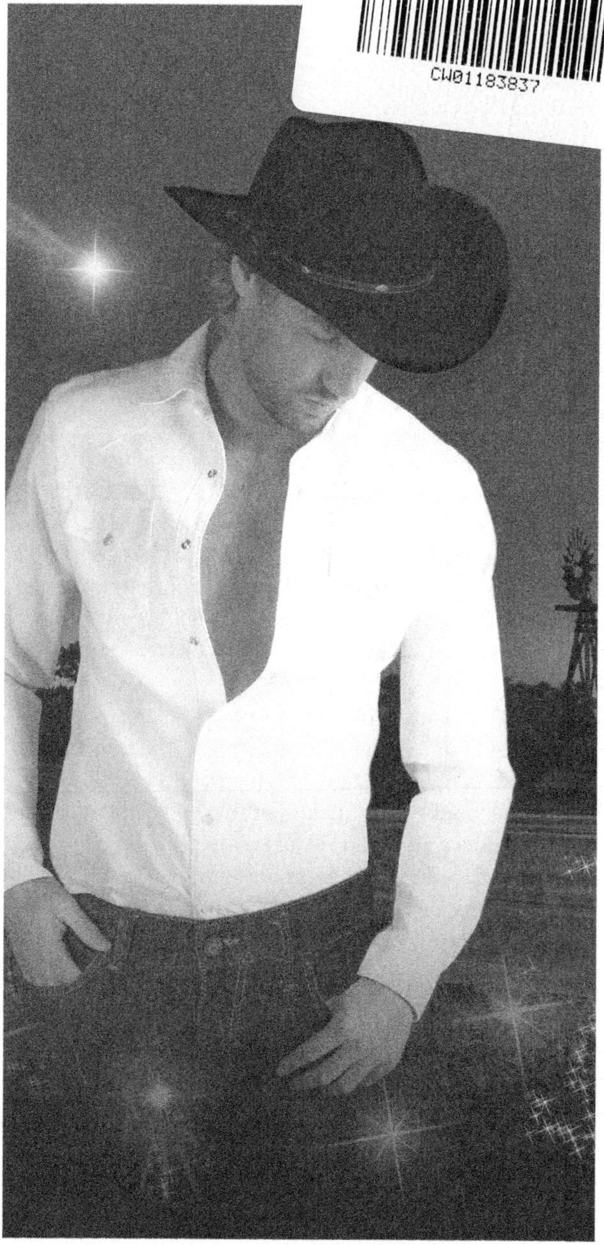

CHARMING A TEXAS PRINCE

Copyright © 2022 by Katie Lane

All rights reserved. Except for use in any review, the reproduction or utilization of this work in whole or in part in any form by any electronic, mechanical or other means, now known or hereinafter invented, including xerography, photocopying and recording, or in any information storage or retrieval system, is forbidden without the written permission of the publisher.

This book is a work of fiction. Names, characters, places, and incidents are a product of the writer's imagination. All rights reserved. Scanning, uploading, and electronic sharing of this book without the permission of the author is unlawful piracy and theft. To obtain permission to excerpt portions of the text, please contact the author at *katie@katielanebooks.com*

Thank you for respecting this author's hard work and livelihood.

Printed in the USA.

Cover Design and Interior Format
© KILLION GROUP INC.

Charming a

TEXAS PRINCE

KINGMAN
RANCH
· 5 ·

KATIE LANE

To my favorite cowgirl witch, Angie Owens

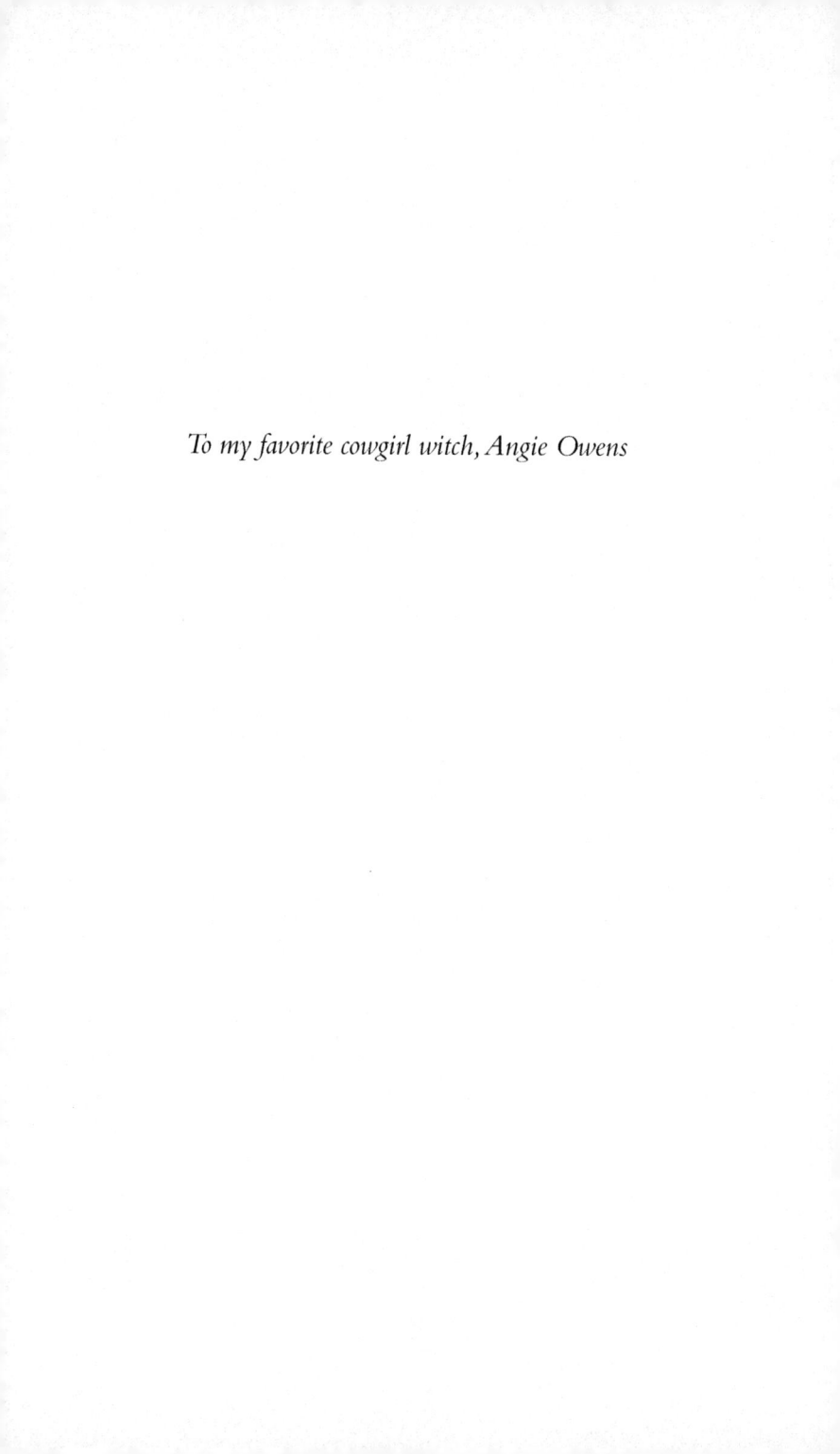

Chapter One

SHE WOULD NEVER ADMIT IT. And if asked, Mystic Twilight Malone would flat out deny that the first Wednesday was her favorite day of the month.

It was just a day like any other day.

She got up at exactly six fifteen. She did yoga for thirty minutes. She meditated for ten minutes more. Then she showered and got dressed. If she took a little extra time picking out her clothes or fixing her hair or applying her makeup, she didn't give it a thought. It was part of her job to look nice for her clients. A hairstylist needed to have style.

Once she was satisfied with the reflection in her mirror, she'd go into the kitchen and make hot tea for her grandmother. There was a specific routine her grandmother had taught her to make the perfect cup of tea. Always use filtered water and loose tea leaves. And always let the tea steep for five minutes.

After pouring water over the infuser filled with leaves, Mystic would set the timer on her smart watch. While waiting, she'd toast an English muffin lightly brown and spread butter into every nook and cranny. By that time, her alarm would go off and she would remove the tea infuser and then carry the cup and the muffin to the small two-person table in the breakfast nook where she would leave it for her grandmother.

Mystic didn't like tea. Or English muffins. She usually just made herself a cup of black coffee. Except on the first Wednesday of every month. On those days, she just sat at the table and stared out the window, waiting for the clock to tick off time.

For some reason, the first Wednesday always turned out to be gorgeous weather. The sun seemed to shine brighter. The rain fell lovelier. The hailstones danced in the grass higher.

Nothing that happened that day could ruin her good mood. It didn't matter if her beauty supply shipment didn't come in. Or a client didn't show up for their appointment. Or her grandmother had caused another problem with the townsfolk of Cursed. Regardless of what happened, the first Wednesday of every month always turned out to be a great day.

Even if her grandmother woke up spouting predictions.

"Tornado's coming."

Mystic continued watching the hummingbirds sipping from the feeder that hung outside the window. Was it her imagination or were the two birds kissing after every drink? She smiled at the thought of kissing hummingbirds.

"Humph. It must be the first Wednesday."

Mystic turned to her grandmother. "What?"

"Nothing." Hester sat down at the table. She was a tall, attractive woman with long silver hair that she refused to let Mystic cut—no matter how much Mystic pleaded. She also refused to wear any color but black—no matter how many brightly colored clothes Mystic gave her for her birthdays and Christmases. The silver hair and black, flowing dresses and skirts only added to the townsfolk's belief that Hester Malone was a witch. And her grandmother's career choice didn't help. Mystic cringed every time she saw the neon sign hanging in the front window of their house.

Fortune-telling and Palm Reading.

Like her ancestors before her, Hester was the town psychic. She read palms and tarot cards and crystal balls and the amethyst hanging from the chain around her neck. If her predictions of doom and gloom weren't accurate 80 percent of the time, people might not believe she was a witch. But Hester was rarely wrong.

"Did you hear me?" Her grandmother picked up her favorite tea mug with the picture of Baby Yoda and the words *Yoda Best Psychic* beneath. "A tornado is coming."

"I heard you." Mystic glanced out the window at the beautiful September day. "But not only is it a gorgeous day, tornado season for Texas is usually May and early June."

Hester added four cubes of sugar to her tea and stirred it six times one way and four times the other before setting the spoon on the right of her cup. "The tornadoes in my dream don't always represent actual tornadoes. You should know that by now, granddaughter."

Mystic more than knew it. Hester hadn't just taught her how to make tea. She'd taught her everything about the psychic world. More than Mystic wanted to know. Her grandmother's dreams, visions, and other psychic abilities had caused Mystic nothing but trouble and alienation from the townsfolk. What Hester viewed as a gift, Mystic viewed as a curse. She wasn't about to give her grandmother validation by entering into a conversation about some dream she had.

"I don't want to talk about dreams, Hessy. That's something *you* should know by now."

Hester slammed her fist on the table, making her tea mug jump. "This isn't a joke, Mystic Twilight! Something bad is going to happen to you. I know it."

"How do you know it? You told me yourself that Malones can't read each other's fortunes or see the future of any blood relative."

"The dream didn't go into detail. It was just a warning. A serious warning." Tears entered her violet eyes. Eyes that Mystic had inherited. "I can't lose you like I lost your mama."

The tears and the mention of Aurora made Mystic realize how upset her grandmother was by the dream. Hester rarely cried and even more rarely talked about her only daughter who had disappeared from both their lives when Mystic was only two years old.

Mystic reached across the table and took

Hester's hand. "Okay. I'm listening. What kind of tornado is coming?"

Hester stroked the amethyst crystal around her neck. "That's just it. I don't know if it's literal or metaphorical. All I saw in my dream was a tornado headed straight for you. Your hair was whipping around your face and you were scared. More scared than I've ever seen you."

She squeezed her grandmother's hand. "If it's an actual tornado, I couldn't work anywhere better than my basement salon. If it's a sign of something that's going to happen in my life, I'll just have to deal with it when it hits."

Hester's eyes grew even more concerned. "That's the problem. You never deal with issues. You just hide from them. Just like your mama did."

"My mama didn't hide. She ran. I'm not a runner, Hessy." If she had been, she would have left a long time ago. Leaving would have made her life so much easier. But she couldn't bring herself to leave Hester. As much as her grandmother annoyed her, Mystic loved her and owed her for being there when her mother hadn't been. "I promise I'll keep my eyes open and take all the precautions I need to if a tornado—real or otherwise—shows up in my life."

"And you'll keep me posted on anything unusual that happens?" Hester asked. "I mean it, Mystic. I can't help you if you continue to keep secrets from me."

She took note of the "continue," but refused to

acknowledge it. She had kept a secret from her grandmother. And everyone else in town.

"I'll keep you posted." She added a silent amendment. *If it's something I think you need to know.* She got up. "Now stop worrying. I'm going to be fine."

"I don't want you to be fine. I want you to be happy."

"I am happy."

Hester shook her head. "You can fool the townsfolk, but you can't fool me. You haven't been truly happy since high school. Something happened back then. Something that took your sparkle away. If there wasn't a psychic block with my own family members, I would've known what it was and I could've helped you." She hesitated. "I still can if you'd tell me."

Mystic thanked God every day for the family psychic block. Hester didn't need to know what had happened. She would be thrilled and spread the news around town. Which would only cause more problems for Mystic.

"There's nothing to tell." She brushed a kiss on Hester's cheek before she grabbed an apple from the bowl on the counter and headed out the front door. As she was coming down the porch steps, her cat, Wish, popped out from beneath the azaleas and greeted her with a loud meow. "There you are," she said as she leaned down to stroke the cat's sleek black fur. "Out carousing again last night, were you?"

Mystic had sworn she would never get another cat after Magic, the black cat her grandmother had given her on her tenth birthday, had died. Not only did she not want to feel the sharp pain of loss again, but she also didn't want to add to the townsfolk's belief that the Malone women were witches. But then Wish had shown up on her doorstep a few months back and she'd been unable to turn the cute little solid black kitten away.

"Come on, " she said. "I'll get you some breakfast."

The cat daintily followed behind her as Mystic headed down the steps to the basement door.

Stepping into the salon always filled Mystic with pride. She had designed every aspect of the salon herself. She'd picked out the striped lavender wallpaper and cushioned purple salon chairs and retro black-and-white checkered tile and the gleaming black shampoo bowls and the shiny chrome fixtures and the lush white lobby couch and each fuzzy throw pillow.

She loved everything about the salon. This was her haven. The place where she wasn't the granddaughter of the town fortune-teller and palm reader. Or the poor parentless Malone girl whose daddy hadn't acknowledged her and whose mama had run off and left her. Here, she was just a prominent businesswoman who had worked hard to get the town's respect. She was damn proud of her accomplishments.

After feeding Wish, she started getting the salon open for business. She set up the appointment software on the computer and arranged the magazines on the coffee table in front of the lobby couch. She pulled the clean towels out of the dryer and folded them before stacking them back in the cupboards over the shampoo bowls. And she swept the floor for any hair she might have missed the night before.

Once everything was ready, she put away the broom and dustpan and glanced at the clock on the wall.

9:07 a.m.

She smiled.

Her first appointment on the first Wednesday of every month was always late. She walked to the mirror at her station and reapplied her favorite brand of red lipstick before she fluffed her short black hair and brushed a fleck of mascara from beneath her eye. She wasn't the fairest one of all, but she would do.

When the bell over the door jingled, her heart rate accelerated. She ignored her heart. Just like she would continue to ignore it for the next hour.

She turned from the mirror as her morning appointment strode in. He wore the light blue T-shirt with the Austin brewpub logo on the front and his favorite pair of faded Wranglers with the worn spot on the right back pocket. His straw cowboy hat was new. His sister Delaney's goat Karl had munched on the last one . . . and the one before that . . . and the one before that. Beneath the curved brim, his familiar blue eyes—a deeper shade of the robin's eggs they'd found together one summer when they had been seven—twinkled back at her.

"Hey, Missy!"

She placed a hand on her hip in faked exasperation. "You're late again, Buck Kingman."

"Sorry. Big brother called me into his office and got after me for being forgetful." He hooked his cowboy hat on the coatrack before he walked over and handed her a takeout cup. "But I didn't forget your coffee."

She took a sip and sighed. "Then you're forgiven."

"You are so easy, Miss." He laughed as he folded his tall frame into the salon chair at her station. "I wish my brother was so easy to appease."

Paying absolutely no attention to the way his muscled body filled the chair, Mystic set down her coffee at her station and took a purple plastic cape from a drawer. She shook it out before placing it around Buck's broad shoulders. The sight of the rough and tough cowboy in a purple cape always made her smile.

"So what did you forget this time?" she asked. Buck had always been disorganized and forgetful. He was lucky he had four older siblings to keep him on track. And Mystic. "I told you to start using your cellphone calendar to give you reminder alerts."

"I know. I know. But I never had to remember to schedule the hay crew. One of my siblings always did that. Now, suddenly, it's my job."

She snapped the cape around his neck, ignoring the feel of the warm skin on the back of his neck. "Your sisters and brothers have other responsibilities now. Like their new spouses."

Buck scowled. "Exactly."

"It sounds a little like you're jealous."

"Hell yeah, I'm jealous. I'm the one in the family who always wanted to get married, and now everyone is married but me. It doesn't seem fair."

Since they'd been in high school, the only thing Buck had ever dreamed about was getting married and having a bunch of kids. At one time, Mystic had wanted the same thing. Now she was quite happy being a single, prosperous businesswoman.

Quite happy.

"Poor Buck," she said as she picked up a comb from her station. "You live in a castle on a hill and can have any woman in town you want, but it's still not enough."

He shot her an annoyed look. "I should've known I wouldn't get any sympathy from you."

"Not a drop." Mystic ran the comb through his hair.

It was the color of moonlight. And in bright sunlight, it almost looked like he wore a glowing halo. But she knew for a fact Buck was no angel. At eight, he'd almost burned the barn down due to his infatuation with matches and fire. At thirteen, he'd stolen Wolfe's girlie magazines and barricaded himself in the tree house for hours. At fifteen, he'd written the answers to his history final on the inside of his arm. At seventeen, he'd had sex with Ginny Myers in her bedroom while her parents were downstairs watching *The Big Bang Theory*. As an adult, he drank, gambled, cussed, and fought when provoked . . . and continued to entertain women in their bedrooms.

No, Buck wasn't an angel. But he was a kind, loyal man who would make some woman a great husband.

Just not her.

She stopped combing his hair and stepped back. "So you want the same cut as always or would you like to try something daring?" She cocked her head and sent him a sassy look in the mirror. "Maybe a mullet? Or I could shave the words 'Marry Me' in the back."

Buck laughed. He had the best laugh. A chortle mixed with a loud guffaw. "If you think it would help, shave away."

"That desperate, are you?"

His laughter quickly died and a sadness entered his blue eyes. "Why can't I find love, Miss? All my siblings have found it and they weren't even looking. I've been looking for years and it's completely avoided me." His gaze held her in its grip. "Am I that ugly?"

Ugly? Buck Kingman was about as far from ugly as a man could get. It wasn't just his blond hair that sprouted from his head like a field of moonlit wheat. Or his straight nose without one bump or freckle to mar it. Or his wide mouth with two even twin peaks on top and a plump full lip on the bottom he chewed on when he got worried. Or his robin's-egg-blue eyes with their long golden lashes. Or the cute little dimple in his left cheek that came out when he smiled his lopsided grin. It was the combination of all those features wrapped in a muscled cowboy's body that made all the women in town breathless. Including her. She had just learned to regulate her breathing when he was around.

She, playfully, tapped him on the head with the comb. "You're not so ugly, Buckaroo. I'm sure some woman somewhere will find you cute enough to fall head over boots in love with you. Now let's get your hair washed. I've got other clients today."

"Gee, thanks for the pep talk, Miss," he said sarcastically as he got up from the chair and followed her to the shampoo bowl.

Once he had reclined in the chair with his head positioned in the curve of the sink, she picked up the sprayer and wet his hair before applying a liberal amount of conditioning shampoo. As soon as she slid her fingers into his hair and started to massage his scalp, his eyes slid closed like they always did.

She glanced at the clock.

This was her moment. The one moment once a month that she let down her guard. The one moment when she stepped across the line drawn in the sand of her heart and let herself feel.

As her fingers stroked through Buck's sudsy strands, her heart quickened and her breath grew uneven and she pretended for a second they were different people. Two strangers with no past and no history. Two strangers who could start all over and, maybe this time, find love.

She only gave herself the minute. No more. And no less. She felt like a minute wasn't too much to ask for. Once it was up, she removed her fingers and rinsed the shampoo.

By the time Buck opened his eyes, all he saw was his smiling best friend.

Chapter Two

A HAIRCUT ALWAYS MADE THINGS FEEL right in Buck's world.

Today was no different.

He'd walked into the salon feeling disheartened about his life, and as he watched Mystic take a snip of his hair before her fingers brushed against his scalp to lift another strand, he felt much better. She was right. There was bound to be some woman somewhere who would be his perfect match. An outdoorsy woman who loved riding horses and fishing. A fun-loving woman who enjoyed a good joke, good beer, and good conversation. An independent woman who would understand the long hours a ranch owner worked and have her own things that kept her busy. An honest woman who wouldn't keep secrets from him.

These were the things he was looking for in a woman. The things he was having trouble finding. If they were fun loving, they didn't understand his long work hours. If they understood his long work hours, they didn't enjoy heading to Nasty Jack's bar for a little drinking and some two-stepping. If they liked to party, they weren't looking for a serious relationship.

Maybe he was being too picky. Maybe he needed to drop some of his requirements and just have one. She couldn't keep secrets. He couldn't live with a woman who didn't share her thoughts and feelings. As far as he was concerned, secrets were what killed his mama. And he'd have none of those in his marriage.

His gaze settled on Mystic's heart-shaped face in the mirror. A face he knew as well as his own. Short feathered hair as black as raven wings. A button nose tilted just a tad at the end. High cheekbones that rarely blushed. Bowed lips that pursed when she was concentrating—like now— and pouted when she was mad. A pointy chin with a tiny scar beneath that she'd gotten from falling down the stairs of the Kingman tree house while chasing Buck.

What had she been mad about? He couldn't remember now. But he did remember how scared he'd been when he saw the blood dripping onto her shirt. He'd carried her all the way back to the house. It hadn't been easy. At ten, she'd been the same size as he was.

She wasn't the same size as he was anymore. The top of her head barely reached his chin and that was while wearing the high-heeled boots she loved. She wore some today with low shanks that barely covered her ankles. The rest of her legs were bare all the way to the hem of her short, flowered dress.

She had nice legs for a petite girl. They were

well shaped and toned from riding horses. Not that she rode anymore. She spent most of her time working at the salon. It was annoying. He missed riding with Mystic. He missed glancing over and seeing her face crinkled with laughter as they raced over Kingman land. He missed fishing with her at the pond and lazing away the last days of summer beneath the big Texas sky.

He just missed her.

"You should come to the ranch this afternoon and we'll go riding," he said abruptly.

Mystic's hands stilled above his head as their gazes caught in the mirror. Her eyes were the most unusual color. A mixture of deep bluebonnet and the lilacs that grew in the garden on the ranch.

She looked away and continued snipping. "Sorry, I have to work late tonight."

"Then come Sunday after church."

"There's a potluck after church and I promised Pastor Chance that I'd help serve."

"Then Monday. You don't open the salon on Mondays."

She set her scissors on the counter and picked up the electric trimmer. "That's my day to do all my accounting and organizing."

He sighed. "I know you've said you aren't avoiding me, Miss, but this sure feels like avoidance."

"I have a business to run, Buck. And unlike you, I don't have four siblings to fall back on." She switched on the trimmers and tipped his head forward a little too forcefully.

But he couldn't blame her for being annoyed. It

wasn't fair that Mystic didn't have anyone to fall back on except her grandmother. It was hard to put much trust in a woman who spent her days reading tea leaves, tarot cards, and palms. While Hester Malone made money on her fortune-telling business, it wasn't enough to pay the bills and put food on the table. Mystic did that. And had done it ever since she'd been old enough to get a job.

Buck, on the other hand, had never had to shoulder the responsibility of taking care of his family. Or even himself. That job had fallen to his oldest brother, Stetson, and his oldest sister, Adeline, after their mother and father had passed away. It was Stetson and Adeline who had carried the weight of keeping the ranch going . . . and their three teenage siblings out of trouble.

It hadn't been an easy job. Wolfe, Delaney, and Buck were rowdy, outspoken, and stubborn. Being owners of the wealthiest ranch in the county made the Kingman kids the princes and princesses of Cursed. As far as the townsfolk were concerned, they could do no wrong—even when they did wrong.

Mystic hadn't been so lucky. As the fortune-teller's granddaughter, she was seen as more of a witch than a princess. Even when she had no psychic powers at all and spent any free time she had giving back to the town by helping out at the church and serving as president of the Cursed Ladies' Auxiliary Club.

It wasn't fair. Not fair at all.

When Mystic finished trimming his neck, Buck

lifted his head and caught her violet eyes in the mirror. "You can fall back on me, Missy."

For one brief, breath-halting moment, their gazes held. Then she looked away and laughed. "Doubtful. You didn't even catch me when I stumbled in my new high heels at the freshman dance. You let me fall right on my butt while you ogled Susie Reed."

"Okay, so that was my bad. But you can't blame me for staring at Susie. Every boy at the dance was distracted by the low-cut dress she wore."

She took off the cape and stood back. "You're all done."

He barely glanced in the mirror as he got to his feet. "Perfect as usual." He pulled out his wallet, even though he knew Mystic wouldn't let him pay.

"Put that right back in your pocket. What are friends for if not to give you a free haircut?" She picked up a shiny red apple from her station and held it out. "And I brought you an apple from our tree. We have a bumper crop this year."

He hesitated. "I seem to remember this scenario from somewhere. An offered apple from a—"

"Don't even go there, Buckaroo." She pulled the apple back. "If you don't want it . . ."

"I want it." He grabbed the apple and took a bite. "A little poison never hurt anyone."

Like always when his haircut was over, he wanted to prolong their time together. But Mystic glanced at the clock and he knew his time was up. He wanted to say something. Something that would fix what had been broken between them. Except he didn't know what was broken. Or how it had gotten broken. All he knew was that somewhere along the way they'd lost the close connection they'd once had.

The door opened and Mildred Pike, who worked at Cursed Market, hurried in. "Hey, y'all! Sorry I showed up without an appointment, Mystic, but I was hoping you could squeeze me in." She held up her long orange claws. "I broke a nail and need it fixed before my date with Jake tonight."

"Jake Taylor?" Mystic asked.

Mildred smiled widely and nodded. "I know. I can't believe that handsome cowboy asked me out. But he did. He just waltzed right up to my cash register with a six-pack of beer and while I was checking him out, he asked if I wanted to hang out with him tonight."

For some reason, Mystic didn't look happy about the news. "Are you sure you want to go out with Jake, Mildred? I think he's still in love with Amy."

Mildred shook her head. "Oh, no. They broke up months ago and Amy's dating Stu Walker."

"That doesn't mean Jake is over her . . . or she is over him."

Mildred stared at her. "What makes you think that? Did Amy say something to you?"

"Well, no, but . . ." Mystic let the sentence drift off before she shook her head. "You're right. If they broke up, they probably aren't still in love. Now let's get that nail fixed for your big date." She glanced at Buck. "See ya next month, Buck."

The thought that he wouldn't get to see her for an entire month didn't sit well with him. Or maybe what didn't sit well was her acting like that was okay. There was a time they had seen each other every day. Now he was lucky if he saw her once a week and he was always the one who had to make the effort. It was starting to really annoy him. But as always, he hid his anger and grabbed his hat off the rack and pulled it on.

"See you, Missy. Enjoy your date with Jake, Mildred."

On the way past the appointment desk, he left a twenty-dollar bill in the tip jar. When he opened the door, a streak of black raced out ahead of him.

Buck had found Wish at an animal shelter in Amarillo two months earlier and left the cat on the Malones' front porch. Mystic had said she didn't want another cat after the cat her grandmother had given her died, but Buck knew she had just been hurting from the loss. Buck knew all about hurting from loss. People thought he'd been too young when his mother passed away to remember her. But you didn't have to have memories to feel the loss of a mother.

When he reached the top of the stairs that led to the basement, the cat was waiting for him. Buck crouched down to give the cat a good scratch. "You keep a close eye on her, Wish."

He straightened and took a few more bites of the apple Mystic had given him before he tossed the core into the fields that ran along the back of the Malones' property. On his way to his truck, he saw Hester sitting in her usual spot on the front porch. While most of the townsfolk were scared of Hester and her weird psychic ability, Buck just saw the woman who had made him and Mystic grape juice popsicles in the stifling summers and hot cinnamon tea in the chilly winters. A woman who had hugged him close when he'd lost his father and told him nice stories about his mother.

Hester might have strange powers, but she also had a good heart.

"Mornin', Hessy! Have you seen any beautiful women in my future yet?" It was a question he asked every time he saw her. Every time, she gave him the same answer.

"Nope. Not a one."

Buck sighed as he climbed the porch steps. "You could make something up, you know? Just to give me a little hope."

"Lies are bad for business."

He laughed as he sat down in the chair next to her. "Fine. If you don't know anything about my future bride, what have you seen?"

Hester patted her lap and Wish jumped onto it. She stroked the cat's fur and stared out at the street. "It's going to be a warm autumn, but a cold winter. We might even get a few inches of snow. And there could be a tornado. Although I'm still not certain about that. Oh, and I've seen a new woman moving to town."

Buck perked up. "A woman? Like a woman my age?"

"Yes. But she's not your woman."

"Are you sure?"

"Positive." She sent him a pointed look. "But I

doubt that's going to stop you from running after her like a dog in heat."

Buck clutched his chest. "A dog? You wound me, Hessy."

"I doubt anything can wound your ego." Her violet eyes grew intent as she continued to pet Wish, who was purring loudly. "And I can tell you one thing. You can't chase love and expect to catch it. Love has to find you."

Before he could say that love had gotten lost when it came to him, a postal truck zipped into the dirt driveway and came to a dust-spitting stop. Kitty Carson jumped out.

Kitty was as short as she was wide with flaming red hair styled in a stiff helmet around her full, friendly face. She had delivered the mail to Cursed and the surrounding ranches ever since Buck could remember. She also delivered the gossip. If something was going on in the town, Kitty knew about it.

Which probably explained why Hester and Kitty didn't get along. Both women thought of themselves as bearers of town news. One told what was happening in the present and the other in the future. They didn't like sharing their spotlights.

Hester got to her feet, causing the cat to jump down. "I thought I told you not to come on my property, Gossip Girl."

"As a postal worker, it is my job to come on people's property, Witchy Woman," Kitty fired back. "And believe me, I wouldn't come near you if I didn't have to." She pulled a box out of the truck. "I'm here on official bid-ness. This is for Mystic. It's postmarked from San Fran and stamped fragile. There's no return address, but seeing as how it's almost Mystic's birthday, I'm sure it's from her mama like all those other boxes were."

Hester visibly bristled and headed down the steps of the porch. Figuring he might need to referee, Buck followed. "It's none of your concern who sends my granddaughter mail," Hester snapped. "Your job is to deliver the mail. Not speculate who it's from." She reached for the package, but Kitty pulled it back.

"The name on the box is Mystic Malone, not Hester Malone. I'd be remiss in my duties if I gave this to the wrong person." Hester's eyes narrowed, and Kitty quickly lifted the box in front of her face. "Don't you dare put a hex on me, Witchy Woman!"

"I'll hex you." Hester waved a hand dramatically. "I'll hex you right out of Cursed."

Buck figured it was time to step in. "Now, ladies, there's no reason to fight over a box." He took the box from Kitty. "I'll make sure Mystic gets this, Miss Kitty. You can get back to your route."

"You I trust, Buck." Kitty shot a mean look at Hester. "Unlike other people in this town." When Hester waved her hand again, Kitty dove into her mail truck and took off.

Once she was gone, Hester lowered her hand and grinned.

Buck laughed and shook his head. "You love scaring the heck out of poor Miss Kitty, don't you?"

"Maybe a little." Hester glanced at the box and her smile faded. Buck knew why. Every year, Aurora sent a box to Mystic on her birthday. Every year, they were postmarked from a different city. Phoenix. Cheyenne. Provo. New Orleans. Atlanta. Chicago. Orlando. It seemed that Aurora Malone was trying to hit every state in the continental United States.

Every one but Texas.

"Maybe it's just hair products," he said. "You know how Mystic loves to order new hair products."

Hester's gaze lifted. "You and I both know what it is, Buck. We also know how upset it's going to make her." She sighed. "Put it up there on the porch. She doesn't need to know about it until she's done working."

Buck hesitated. "Maybe she doesn't need to know about it at all. I could easily dispose of it."

"You can't dispose of pain that easily." Hester shook her head. "No, Mystic has to learn how to deal with it."

Buck didn't want Mystic to have to deal with it. He wanted her mama to stop pouring salt into Mystic's wounds. If Hester hadn't been standing there watching, he would have taken the box to his truck and thrown it out the window as he drove along the highway. Instead, he grudgingly carried the box up the steps of the porch and set it by the door.

When he turned, Hester was standing behind him. "She'll need you after she opens it."

Buck nodded. "I'll be here for her."

Until the day he died, he always would be.

Chapter Three

THREE LOAVES OF SOURDOUGH BREAD. Mystic hated sourdough bread. A bag of Ghirardelli dark chocolates. She preferred milk chocolate. A trio of scented candles. Okay, so she loved scented candles. But an *I Love San Francisco* hoodie? As if she'd ever wear that in Texas. And a birthday card in a bright pink envelope with a unicorn on it, as if Mystic was still ten.

Mystic hadn't opened the card to see if it had unicorns too. She had stopped opening the birthday cards her mother sent on her ninth birthday when she'd learned the definition of hypocrisy was two words—"Love, Mom." That year, the package had been postmarked in Orlando and held a Snow White dress, a cute stuffed Dumbo, and beach flip-flops.

Every item had ripped Mystic's heart in two. Because what little girl doesn't dream of walking toward Cinderella's castle wearing a princess dress while holding her mama's hand? Or soaring through the air on the Dumbo ride tucked against her mama's side? Or racing against the ocean tide with her glittery flip-flops in her hand and her mama close on her heels?

Mystic had destroyed everything in the box that year. She had ripped up the Mickey Mouse card. Cut the dress into tiny satin pieces. She had gutted poor Dumbo and slashed holes in the rubber thongs. Then she'd put the riddled debris back in the box and carried it outside where she set the entire thing on fire while Hester watched from the second-floor window of her bedroom. Her grandmother had never said a word, but her sadness had been easy to read.

Not wanting to upset her grandmother again, Mystic had handled the birthday boxes differently after that. She would open the box, dispassionately look at the contents, throw away any food items, then carry what was left up to the attic where she'd stack the box with the other boxes. There were now seventeen boxes tucked beneath the eaves of the old house. Minus the boxes she'd kept before she turned nine, the burned box, and Mystic's first and second birthdays—the only birthdays Aurora had spent with Mystic.

Not that Mystic remembered her mother. Everything she knew about Aurora had come from stories Hester told her and old pictures.

Aurora had been a wild child. Or as Hester referred to her, "a free spirit." She had embraced the town's label of being a witch and had worn all black like Hester with the Goth touch of black lipstick and nail polish. On her sixteenth birthday, Aurora had been overjoyed to get her psychic sight.

But her dream wasn't to become a fortune-teller in a small town. She'd had bigger dreams. At eighteen, she left for Los Angeles where she became a telephone psychic. Her success at reading people's deepest desires and seeing into their future made her extremely popular. Soon she had her own psychic business and was offering love and life advice to the California elite. Unfortunately, she couldn't see into her own future or she wouldn't have fallen for a deadbeat bass player and gotten married. Two years later, she returned to Cursed.

But only to drop off her daughter.

"Missy?"

Mystic startled out of her thoughts and turned to the opening in the attic. A straw cowboy hat appeared first, followed by Buck's familiar blue eyes. She rushed to stop him from coming any farther. She didn't want him seeing the boxes stacked in the corner. He knew about the birthday boxes. He just didn't know she had kept them all. It was foolish. But for some reason, she just couldn't throw them away. Sadly, she even regretted destroying her ninth birthday box.

"No need to come up," she said. "I'll come down. It's a dusty mess up here."

But Buck didn't listen. He never listened. Before she could start down the ladder, he was standing in the attic hunched beneath the eaves.

"How come I've never been up here? This is badass." He glanced around and his eyes lit up. "Is that your old spring horse? Damn, I loved that thing. Remember how we used to climb on it together and the horse's hooves brushed the floor as we galloped away from the posse chasing us after we'd robbed the cookie jar?"

"All I remember is how you tried to buck me off."

He grinned. "But you never let me. You always held on tight."

He continued to peruse the contents of the attic. She knew the second his gaze fell upon the neatly stacked boxes tucked in the corner. His smile faded and a sad look entered his eyes. Thankfully, it was gone quickly. That was the thing she loved most about Buck. He didn't let anything keep him down. He always released sadness quickly and kept moving forward.

"Look at that old sewing machine," he said. "That has to be worth something. And is that a crystal ball? I thought Hessy keeps hers downstairs."

"That's not Hester's. It's my great-great-grandmother's. Every fortune-teller must use their own crystal ball. If anyone even touches Hessy's, she places it in a tub of sea salt overnight to cleanse it from outside energy or influences." Mystic rolled her eyes. "I have an entire family of nuts."

"Now don't start putting down your family. You have to admit Hester gets some things right."

"If you make enough predictions, you're bound to get something right."

"She gets quite a few things right. I think you're just mad because you don't have the sight." His eyes twinkled. "Or maybe you have it and you just haven't practiced enough." He moved closer. "Go ahead, Missy. Look into my eyes and try to tell me what I'm thinking."

It was something he had asked her to do ever since they were kids. When they were younger, she would stare into his eyes and try as hard as she could to read his thoughts. She stopped trying after her sixteenth birthday. After she realized she'd fallen in love with Buck Kingman and he didn't return that love.

One night, they'd been lying in the hayloft looking at the stars when Buck had turned to her and asked her to read his thoughts. She couldn't read his thoughts, but looking into his familiar blue eyes, she suddenly realized that she had fallen in love with him. Fallen in love with his teasing smile and his boyish good looks. Fallen in love with his fun-loving personality and kind heart.

If she had been an ordinary girl, she might've confessed her love. But she wasn't ordinary. Like all the other Malone women, on her sixteenth birthday, she'd been given a gift. Or a curse. She could read people's emotions. Not just any emotions, but love. At first, she had just thought she was good at reading facial expressions. But she soon realized that even if people weren't looking at her, she could see a golden aura around them when they looked at certain people.

That night in the hayloft, there had been no aura around Buck when he'd looked at her. There had just been the same love she'd always seen in his eyes. The friendship kind of love they held now.

She looked away and answered his question. "You're hungry and want to know what Hester made for supper."

He laughed. "You got it half right. I am hungry, but I'm not wondering what Hester made for supper. She already told me. Nothing. It's leftover night. So I thought you and I would head on over to Nasty Jack's for dinner and a slice of Gretchen's pie."

"I'm afraid I—"

He held up his hand and cut her off. "I'm not accepting no for an answer, Missy. If I have to, I'll pick you up and carry you to Nasty's."

Her eyes widened. "You most certainly will not."

His eyebrows lifted beneath the brim of his pushed-up hat. "Wanna bet?" He made a grab for her, but she ducked under his arm.

The chase was on.

Buck might be bigger and stronger, but she was smaller and quicker. In a cluttered attic, that worked in her favor. She moved around the trunks, old furniture, and boxes with ease while he bumped into things like a bear in a china cabinet. When he bumped into a dress mannequin and knocked it over, she took the opportunity to head for the ladder. She made it to the bottom, but he was hot on her heels. She raced toward the front door with a plan to head to her salon and lock him out. But he caught up with her in the yard. Sure enough, he scooped her off her feet with one arm and flung her over his shoulder.

"Put me down, Buck!" she yelled as she

struggled to get out of his arms—his strong, muscled arms. When had he gotten all the flexing muscles?

"I plan to. Just as soon as we get to Nasty Jack's." He walked past the porch. "Night, Hessy!"

Mystic lifted her head and saw her grandmother standing on the porch. "Aren't you going to stop him, Hessy?" she yelled.

"Nope," her grandmother answered. "You need a night out. Keep a close eye on her, Buck."

"Yes, ma'am. We all know what happens when Missy has too many beers. I promise I won't let her dance on the bar tonight."

"You dared me!" she snapped indignantly. Although it was hard to be indignant when you were hanging upside down. "I mean it, Buck. Put me down. My panties are showing."

"Well, we can't have that." But instead of putting her down, he reached up and tugged down the hem of her dress, his warm fingers brushing against one butt cheek and the top of her thigh. A rush of heat slammed into her and left her too stunned to protest further. She hung there limply as Buck carried her across the street to the bar.

Nasty Jack's was owned by Buck's great-uncle Jack, but run by Buck's brother Wolfe and his wife, Gretchen. Although now that Gretchen was pregnant, Wolfe was looking high and low for someone to take over running the bar's kitchen. But it wasn't easy to find help in a small town. Mystic had been looking for a stylist to help her at the salon since she'd opened it.

The bar was packed tonight—as it was most

nights. If people weren't there for a beer, they were there for Gretchen's tasty pies. And their gossip Spidey sense would be on full alert if Buck carried Mystic into the bar. Thankfully, he set her down before they reached the door. His eyes were no longer teasing. They were pleading.

"Please stay, Miss."

She had never been able to ignore a plea from Buck. "Fine. But only for an hour."

A smile lit his face. "Just an hour . . . or maybe two." He pulled the door open for her. Once inside, he placed a hand on her back and guided her through the crowd. A cowboy sitting at the bar saw them and greeted Buck.

"Hey there, Buck! You're here just in time to buy me a beer."

Buck grinned. "You betcha, Mitch." He leaned over the bar and yelled to his brother, who was busy mixing drinks. "Hey, Wolfe, give our new ranch hand, Mitch, a beer on me. And one for me and Mystic."

Wolfe finished handing a margarita to a woman at the end of the bar before he filled two glasses with beer and brought them over and set them in front of Buck. "Those are for you and Mystic. Mitch will pay for his own beer." His sharp gaze zeroed in on Mitch. "I heard you were napping on the job."

"Now, Wolfe," Buck said. "I'm sure Mitch didn't mean any harm." He looked at Mitch. "Did you?"

If the smirk on Mitch's face was any indication, he didn't feel the least bit regretful about his actions. "When I worked in Mexico, I always had an afternoon siesta." He shrugged. "But if the Kingmans have something against a man getting a little rest after working hard, I guess I'll have to change my habits." He got up and tipped his hat at Buck. "I'll get that beer another time, Buck."

When he was gone, Wolfe turned to Buck. "You need to fire him."

"For what? Wanting a free beer?"

"No, for sleeping on the job and still thinking you'd buy him a beer. And it's your own fault. You don't act like a boss so therefore you don't get treated like one. You can't be everyone's friend, Buck." He winked at Mystic. "Isn't that right, baby girl?"

Mystic took the barstool Mitch had vacated. "Don't try to get me on your side with your flirty ways, Wolfe Kingman. I became immune to your charming smiles and winks when I had to endure your and Buck's farting competitions."

Wolfe laughed. "If I remember correctly, you and Del won more than your fair share of those."

Before Mystic could argue the point, a cowboy down the bar yelled for a beer and Wolfe left to get it. When he was gone, Buck's smile faded.

"Am I too friendly with the ranch's employees?"

Mystic wasn't surprised by the question. Buck might act like he didn't care what his siblings thought of him, but he took everything they said to heart.

She placed a hand on his arm. "There's nothing wrong with being nice, Buck. But maybe you do need to act more like a boss and less like their friend."

"It's hard to act like a boss when you're never gotten the chance to be one." He took a long drink of his beer before he continued. "I'll bet you money that Wolfe fires Mitch before the week is out. Not one of my siblings trusts me to make decisions."

He had a good point. Buck didn't stand a chance of being a boss when he was the easygoing one of the family. The one who didn't care about being in charge.

The hurt in his eyes cut right through her. She squeezed his arm. "They trust you, Buck. It's just hard for them to let you be the boss when you've always been their little brother."

He sighed. "And yet they expect me to act like the boss. You can't ever learn to make decisions if people don't let you make them. Maybe that's why I can't decide on a wife."

"I don't think finding a wife is a decision you make, Buck. It's just something that happens."

He turned those bright blue eyes on her. "Why won't it happen for me, Miss?"

It was a question she had asked God more times than she could count. Why couldn't Buck fall in love with her? Why couldn't she be the one to surround him in golden light? The one to give him a castle full of moonlight-haired children?

She'd never gotten an answer to her questions. Maybe because she knew the answer. A cowboy prince didn't belong with the town witch. He belonged with a princess. Someone who wasn't cursed with psychic powers. Or a family who collected crystal balls. Unable to sit there and look into Buck's sad eyes a second longer—or discuss the reason he couldn't find love—Mystic got to her feet.

"I think I'll go get us some pie."

On the way to the kitchen, she saw Delaney taking an order from a couple of cowboys. Her new husband, Shane, sat at a nearby table, seemingly working on his laptop. But Mystic could tell he wasn't working as much as watching Delaney . . . surrounded by a golden glow. The sight made Mystic feel even more depressed. Were all Malone women destined to loveless lives? Her grandfather hadn't loved Hessy enough. Her father hadn't loved her mother enough.

And Buck didn't love her enough.

Frustrated, she flung open the door to the kitchen a little harder than necessary. It clanged against a serving cart and startled Gretchen who was rolling out piecrust at the prep island.

"Sweet Lord!" She held a hand to her rounded stomach.

Mystic felt instantly contrite. "I'm so sorry, Gretchen. I didn't mean to startle you."

"No worries. I've always startled easily." Gretchen placed a hand on her back and stretched. "I'm glad you stopped in. I needed a little break." She looked like she needed more than a little break. She looked exhausted.

"Let me help." Mystic headed to the sink to wash her hands.

"Thank you." Gretchen sat down on a stool and sighed. "I don't have morning sickness, but I sure have evening tiredness."

Mystic dried her hands and grabbed an apron. "Have you had any luck finding someone to help you in the kitchen?"

"Otis and Thelma have agreed to help out on Fridays and Saturdays now that their daughter and grandkids moved to Austin." Otis and Thelma Davenport ran the Good Eats diner in town. "But that won't be enough when Maribelle comes."

Mystic stared at Gretchen. "Maribelle?"

A big smile bloomed on Gretchen's freckled face. "It's a girl. We're going to have a little girl. Wolfe wants to name her Maribelle because that's my middle name."

Mystic hurried over and hugged her friend. "Oh, Gretchen, that's wonderful news."

Gretchen drew back with tears in her eyes. "It is, isn't it? I never thought that Wolfe would be over the moon about a baby, but he is. And even more surprisingly, so is my mama. Delilah never acted much like she loved being a mother so I thought she wouldn't be excited about becoming a grandma. But I guess those two things are completely different. As soon as I told her I was having a baby girl, she started talking about all the things she wanted to do with her new granddaughter and all the things she and Grandpa Bill wanted to buy her."

"Grandpa Bill?"

Gretchen nodded. "It looks like my mama is getting married once again." Gretchen's mother was addicted to weddings. Just not marriage. As if reading her thoughts, Gretchen laughed. "I know. But she says that this time is different. And it does seem to be different. Her last four husbands had money. This guy has no money and a bad habit of going from one job to the next."

Her forehead knotted. "Which has me a little concerned. I know Mama married for money, but I guess I don't want the same thing happening to her. Not that she doesn't deserve it for all the times she ran out on a man. But she's still my mama and I hate to see her get hurt." She hesitated and nibbled on her bottom lip. "Which is why I was wondering if maybe I could bring Bill and Mama by the salon when they come into town and you could tell me if you think he truly loves her."

Mystic tried not to let her surprise show. "How would I know if he truly loves your mother?"

Gretchen blushed as red as her hair. "Umm . . . well, I guess you wouldn't." She forced a laugh. "Silly me. Now I better get back to rolling out that piecrust." She got up and quickly changed the subject. "So how's business at the salon?"

Mystic made small talk as she helped Gretchen fill more pie tins with crust and filling, but inside she couldn't help wondering how Gretchen had found out about her psychic powers. Since there was only one person who knew the truth, there was only one person to blame.

When Delaney strutted in the door, spouting pie orders, Mystic couldn't help grabbing her arm and pulling her right back out.

"What's going on?" Delaney asked as Mystic dragged her through the bar to the women's bathroom. "Do you need a tampon? Because if you do, I'll have to get my purse behind the bar."

"I don't need a tampon." Mystic waited to say anything else until they were inside the bathroom and she'd checked under every stall door. When she was convinced they were alone, she turned on Delaney.

"Did you tell Gretchen about my secret?" Delaney's guilty look was all the answer she needed. "How could you, Del? You promised."

"I know, but she was so worried about her mama getting married to a man who doesn't love her and I was just trying to ease her fears by telling her that you can tell if people are in love. And she promised not to tell a soul that you're a love psychic."

A gasp had them turning to the last stall. The door swung open and Kitty Carson stepped out with a stunned look on her face.

"You're a love psychic?"

Chapter Four

The dream varied over the years. Sometimes they'd have sex in the hayloft with a curtain of stars above them. Sometimes they had sex on a blanket by the pond with the sun warming their bare skin. And sometimes they would have it in Buck's big ol' king-sized bed amid the soft pillows and crisp sheets.

But after his haircut, it was always at the salon. In the shampoo recliner. In the hydraulic swivel salon chair. On the appointment counter. On the white lobby couch. Against all the walls.

When he was a teenager and in his early twenties, he thought nothing of sex dreams. They were just brought on by raging hormones. Over the years, he'd had sex dreams about a lot of girls, including models, actresses, and the widow Mrs. Swartz.

But lately, he only dreamed about one girl.
Mystic.
And it was starting to freak him out.
Mystic was his friend. His best friend. Waking up after the dreams with a boner that could pound railroad stakes made him feel like some

kind of a sexual pervert. He'd known Mystic for most of his life. She was as close, if not closer, to him than his own sisters.

They met the first day of kindergarten. On the playground, a few punky kids had started picking on Mystic for being the granddaughter of a witch. Buck had never liked people getting picked on. So he'd shoved the head bully and made him apologize. That same day, Mystic had shared her pencils and crayons with him and Delaney because their daddy had forgotten to get their school supplies.

Douglas Kingman had been a poor excuse for a father. He had been more concerned with having affairs with every woman in town than with raising his children. Buck tried to remember if he'd been a better father when Buck's mother had been alive, but he couldn't remember life before his mother passed.

It hurt not being able to remember his mom. But at least he knew his mother hadn't left him on purpose. The car crash had been a horrible accident. Unlike Mystic's mom who had dropped her off like an unwanted puppy. Knowing your mom didn't want you had to be hard.

The proof of Mystic's pain was stacked in her attic.

When Buck had seen all those postal boxes tucked neatly between the rafters it had broken his heart. And yet here he lay with a huge boner. What kind of uncaring friend was he? Instead of having sexual dreams about Mystic, he should be thinking of ways to ease her pain.

With a disgusted snort, he rolled out of bed and headed to the shower. A few minutes in the cold spray was enough to soften his hard-on and get the images of salon sex out of his head. But as he toweled off and got dressed, he couldn't stop thinking about the birthday boxes.

Mystic might act like she didn't care about her mother, but it was obvious she still did. She'd been so upset about the damn birthday box she hadn't even stayed at Nasty Jack's long enough to eat. After she came back from the kitchen, she'd downed her beer in three gulps and left.

But how could he help Mystic get over her mother's desertion?

He was still thinking about the problem when he headed down to breakfast. Ever since their father had died and Stetson had taken over the ranch, Stetson insisted breakfast and dinner be eaten as a family. He got extremely pissed if people didn't follow the rule. But then Wolfe started helping Uncle Jack out with Nasty Jack's bar and couldn't be there for dinners. Adeline got morning sickness and missed numerous breakfasts. Then Lily got morning sickness. Gretchen didn't have morning sickness, but she helped Wolfe out at the bar. Finally, Stetson had given up trying to hold the family together at mealtimes.

Strangely, once the rule was dropped, everyone made more of a point to be together for meals. Every family member was sitting at the table when Buck walked into the kitchen.

Stetson sat at the head of the table with Lily on his right and Uncle Jack on his left. Next to

Uncle Jack sat Wolfe and Gretchen. Adeline sat on the end opposite Stetson with Gage sitting on her right and Delaney and Shane next to him. Since Potts was getting older, Stetson had started insisting he join them for meals and let everyone serve themselves. Which left no room for Buck.

If all his siblings getting married didn't make him feel like a spare part, mealtime certainly did.

But as always, he tried not to act like it mattered as he turned around and walked into the dining room to grab a chair. He usually squeezed in next to Delaney. There was nothing that started his day better than squabbling with his twin. But today Delaney seemed to be in a whispered conversation with Shane so Buck squeezed in between Gretchen and Adeline. When he realized what they were talking about, he wished he'd chosen another spot.

"I swear I pee every two seconds," Adeline complained. "And if that's not enough, my swollen feet look like Fred Flintstone's." Gage laughed, but then quickly sobered when Adeline glared at him. "You think it's funny, Gage Reardon?"

"No, sweetheart, I do not." Gage brushed a kiss on her cheek. "Tonight I'll be happy to rub your Flintstone feet. The pee thing I can't help you with. But it won't be much longer."

Adeline's scowl didn't soften. "Really? You keep saying that, but I'm over a week late and there's no sign this baby is ever coming."

"I read that first babies are always late," Gretchen said. "That little dumplin' will get here. He's just not ready to get out of his cozy mama's belly."

"Well, his mama is more than ready for him to get out." Adeline leaned back in the chair and sighed. "I feel like an overinflated balloon." Her big stomach did look like it was ready to pop. Buck only hoped it didn't pop before he got some breakfast.

He loaded up his plate with Potts's famous French toast casserole and dug in. As he was eating, he continued to think about how to help Mystic. Maybe he should ask Adeline for some advice. Addie had always been levelheaded and he respected her opinion. She was the only mother he'd known. When she'd found out Daddy had forgotten to get his and Delaney's school supplies, she'd rushed to the store and purchased them. When they needed new shoes or a winter coat, it had been Addie who had made sure they had them. She had bandaged their scraped knees, packed their lunches, tucked them in at night, and basically become their mother. She would know how to help Mystic.

After breakfast was over and everyone had headed in different directions, Buck followed her into the sunroom. "Could I talk to you for a second, Addie?"

"Of course." She eased down on the couch and patted the cushion next to her. "What's up?"

He sat down and proceeded to tell his sister about the birthday boxes. When he finished, Adeline's eyes held tears and he instantly regretted his decision to ask her advice. "I'm sorry, Addie. I didn't mean to upset you. Especially when you're pregnant."

"I'm fine. I cry at the drop of a hat now. But it's just so sad that Mystic doesn't want anything in the boxes, but still can't throw them away. Of course, I understand. Having lost our mama, you should too."

"I do. But our mom didn't intentionally leave us. And we don't keep getting packages in the mail to remind us of our loss."

Adeline sighed. "It has to be painful. But maybe Aurora is suffering too."

"Then why doesn't she call Mystic or come back and see her? Why does she just keep sending the damn boxes once a year?"

"Maybe it's her way of saying she loves Mystic— even though she isn't a good mother."

Buck slammed his fist on the couch cushion. "That's horseshit!"

Adeline hooked an arm around his shoulders and pulled him close. He was much bigger than she was, but she still cuddled him as if he were three and brushed a kiss on his head.

"Sometimes the truth is shit. As much as we want to help other people deal with their truth, we can't. They have to deal with it on their own. Mystic will have to come to terms with her mama's desertion in her own way. All you can do is be there for her."

Buck nodded against Adeline's shoulder. "I know, but it's damn hard to watch."

"It's always hard to watch the ones we love suffer."

"Who's suffering?" Delaney stepped into the

room. "And stop babying Buck, Addie. He's a big enough wussy as is."

Buck drew away from Adeline and started to argue the point, but Adeline spoke. "We were talking about Mystic. She got another birthday box from her mama and Buck is worried about her."

"He's always worried about Mystic. He needs to stop worrying about her and start worrying about the ranch." Delaney sent Buck an annoyed look. "You said you'd be willing to take over the horse breeding so I could start my animal refuge. But when I went to the stables today, Tab says you haven't set up any breeding schedule at all. Instead, you're sitting here whining about Mystic. You need to marry the woman, then maybe we could get some work out of you."

Buck laughed. "Like I told you before, Mystic and I are just friends."

Delaney rolled her eyes. "Sure you are. That's why you get a haircut every single month whether you need one or not. Why you look like a dog on bath day when she can't hang out with you. Why you blew a fuse the time she was going to cut Shane's hair."

"There's nothing wrong with scheduling a monthly haircut. Or being upset when your best friend can't hang out with you. As for not wanting her to cut Shane's hair, that was all about you, Del. I knew you liked Shane and were jealous." He looked at Adeline. "Tell her, Addie."

He thought Adeline would take his side. But instead of taking his side, she took Delaney's.

"You do seem to be preoccupied with Mystic."

"Because she's my friend and I care about her. But just because I care about her doesn't mean I should marry her. And if anyone should know that, Addie, you should after what happened between you and Danny."

As soon as the words were out, Buck wanted them back. Adeline and Danny had been childhood friends who had made the mistake of letting things get too serious. It wasn't until they were engaged that Adeline realized her feelings for Danny weren't the marriage kind. She'd broken up with him. Only days later, he had been killed in Afghanistan. Adeline had spent the next year blaming herself for his death.

"I'm sorry, Addie," he said. "I shouldn't have mentioned Danny."

She shook her head. "I can talk about Danny without falling apart. And you're right. I do understand childhood friendships and how emotions can become confused. Mine certainly became confused with Danny." She studied him with a concerned look. "I hope what happened to me hasn't made you leery of getting closer to Mystic."

"Of course not." But it hadn't hurt. He didn't want to be the lovesick fool who fell head over heels for someone who didn't return his love. He didn't want to be Danny. And he sure as hell didn't want to be his mother. He wanted a woman who felt the same way about him as he felt about her.

Mystic had made it perfectly clear that all she felt for Buck was friendship.

"Mystic and I are friends," he said. "Just friends."

Delaney snorted. "Whatever you say, little brother. Now get your ass out to the stables and set up a breeding—"

Adeline cut her off. "Oh!"

Delaney and Buck turned to her. Her eyes were wide and she held her stomach. Buck grew instantly concerned.

"Are you okay, Addie?"

Delaney moved closer. "Of course she's not okay. She's having a contraction. Hang tough, Addie. I'm going to go get Gage."

For a pregnant woman in the midst of a contraction, Adeline moved fast. She grabbed the front of Delaney's shirt and held her tight. "No! You'll do no such thing, Del. If you do, he'll want to head to the hospital. And I won't be stuck in some hospital bed for fourteen hours. Gage and I don't need to head to the county hospital until the contractions are five minutes apart for an hour or longer. Now take out your phone, Buck, so we can time them."

If Adeline hadn't been taking online college courses to become a veterinarian, Buck might have ignored her and gone to get Gage. But she'd helped with numerous births around the ranch and knew much more than he did about delivering babies. So he did what she asked. Once he showed her the time, she relaxed back against the cushions.

"Keep talking, y'all. I need something to take my mind off the contractions."

Buck was too nervous to talk so Delaney did

most of the talking. She talked about Shane, her new animal refuge, Wolfe's stud cutting horse, and Glory Boy, a thoroughbred colt the family had high hopes for. While she talked, Buck watched Adeline's face. When her eyes widened and she tensed, he glanced at his phone. He stopped glancing at his phone when Delaney brought up what had happened in the bathroom the night before.

"I always knew Kitty loved gossip, but I never thought she'd hide in a bathroom stall to hear it. Mystic checked under every stall before she started yelling at me for giving away her secret. So Kitty would've had to pull up her feet. Can you believe the extremes the woman will go to for gossip?"

Buck stared at his sister in confusion. And not because Kitty had hidden in a stall. "What secret?"

"Sorry, little bro, I can't tell you. I don't want Mystic yelling at me again. Although you'll probably find out soon enough. I'm sure Kitty has already spread it all over town."

"Spread what, Del?"

Before Delaney could answer him, Adeline gasped. "Maybe you should go get Gage, Buck." She smiled weakly. "I think my water just broke."

Concern for his sister had Buck forgetting all about Mystic's secret as he raced out the door to find Gage. For a cool and collected ranch foreman, Gage did not handle the news well. He went into pure panic mode and Buck was the one who ended up driving him and Adeline to the hospital.

The rest of the family met them there. Amid all the excitement of a new Kingman being born—Daniel Gage, who came in at a whopping nine pounds and two ounces—Buck didn't remember Mystic's secret until he was on his way back to the ranch.

He wasn't too concerned. He probably already knew what the secret was. If he didn't, it was probably something simple. She was going to add a new service to her salon menu. Or she had thought up a new way for the ladies of the auxiliary club to raise money. Mystic would never keep anything major from him. Best friends didn't keep secrets. In fact, he and Mystic had even taken a blood oath when they were twelve to always tell each other everything.

Still, when he got to Cursed, he decided to pull in and ask her about it.

But before he even reached the Malones' house he saw a line of people standing from the front door all the way out to the street. He had never seen so many people wanting to have their fortunes read. Curious, he pulled over and rolled down his window to talk to the couple standing at the end of the line.

"Hey, Mo, what's going on? Is Hester giving out free readings?"

"This line ain't for Hester," Mo said. "It's for something much worse than a forecast about the weather."

His longtime girlfriend, Trisha, thumped him hard in his beer belly. "Hush up, Mo Davidson. I've been wondering why you haven't proposed for the last two years and tonight I'm finally going to get an answer." She glanced at Buck. "You might want to join us, Buck. Although seeing as how your best friend is a love psychic, I don't know why you haven't found your true love yet."

Chapter Five

Mystic had been right. Her psychic powers didn't turn out to be a gift. They turned out to be a curse. And she was now in hell. Half the town was camped out on her front porch and lawn. The other half kept calling her cellphone and leaving messages requesting her help with their love life or the love life of a family member or friend. After an hour of listening to the phone and doorbell ring, she finally turned off her phone and stuffed cotton balls into the chimes of the doorbell. But once the doorbell stopped working, people started knocking and yelling through the door.

"I just want to know if love is in my future!"

"I think she loves me, but I want to be sure before I spend money on an engagement ring!"

"He says he's not interested in going out with me, but I think he just doesn't know his own mind!"

"My Chihuahua has been acting strange. I think she might be in love with my cat!"

While Mystic paced the floor in the kitchen and tried to figure out how to fix this mess, Hester sat in her favorite overstuffed chair in the family room, drinking Diet Coke and eating popcorn as she watched the movie *Hocus Pocus*. A movie she started watching as soon as September arrived. When it ended, she turned off the television and carried her can and bowl into the kitchen.

"You think pacing is going to fix the problem?"

"I can't sit still when half the town is camped out on our doorstep." Mystic drew back the blinds covering the window over the sink and peeked out. There weren't as many people as there had been before, but there was still a line down the steps of the porch. She sighed and let the blind fall closed.

"Stop fretting," Hester said. "They'll get tired of waiting and go home eventually. People have no patience in this town."

Mystic turned to her. "But what about tomorrow? And the next day? And the day after that? Even if they finally stop coming to the house, I won't be able to leave without them stopping me on the street for a psychic reading."

"They don't stop me on the streets."

"Because they're scared of you. They aren't scared of me. They're my friends."

Hester shrugged. "And whose fault is that?"

Mystic's eyes widened. "It's my fault that I wanted to have friends? My fault that I don't want to be a social outcast like you and Mama? I didn't want this. I never wanted this. I don't want to read people's minds or futures. I just want to be a normal person."

Hester looked thoroughly confused. "Now why in the world would you want that?"

The stress of the day had Mystic's temper snapping. "Because normal people have normal lives! They make friends and fall in love and have families. They don't end up a sad woman who couldn't keep a man or her daughter." As soon as the words were out, she wanted them back. But it was too late. She might not be able to read her grandmother's emotions psychically, but she could read the hurt expression on her face. "I'm sorry, Hessy," she said. "I'm just upset."

Hester nodded. "I understand. Having a gift isn't easy. Especially in a small, judgey town. Your mama couldn't do it." She hesitated. "And maybe you won't be able to either. That's something we'll both have to come to accept."

Mystic stared at her. "Are you saying I might have to leave?"

"I'm saying you'll need to make some tough decisions. I don't want you considering me when you make those decisions. What you decide to do shouldn't be about me. It should be about what makes you happy. Maybe this happened for a reason. Maybe this is what you needed to push you toward your life."

"My life is my salon."

Hester shook her head. "That's where you've gotten things mixed up. Your salon is your job. You should love your job. But you should never mistake it for your life. A life is something to live. A job is something that facilitates that living."

"And what about you, Hessy? Have you lived?"

"I've lived the life I was meant to live. I've been in love once. I've been in lust too many times to count. I've raised a daughter and had my heart broken. I've raised a granddaughter who healed that heart. And through it all I've helped a lot of people prepare for bad times and good. I'd say that has been a life well lived."

Her violet eyes welled with tears. "I wish I could prepare you. I wish I could see what pitfalls you need to avoid and what mountains you'll need to climb. But I can't see your future. What I can see is a strong, intelligent, beautiful woman who I know can get through whatever hardships come her way. And if that means you need to leave Cursed, then that's what you'll need to do. Maybe this was the tornado I saw coming. Maybe these strong winds will take you where you need to go." She paused. "Or maybe they'll just show you where you need to stay."

"Or maybe a house will drop on me and the new witch of Cursed will be gone," she muttered.

Hester chuckled. "Cursed is a lot like Oz—filled with a bunch of people living in a fantasy world. Now let's turn off the lights and go upstairs. Hopefully, if those idiots think we've gone to bed, they'll head on home."

Mystic helped her grandmother turn off the lights before they headed upstairs. When they reached Hester's room, she pulled Mystic into her arms. "It will all work out the way it's supposed to, Mystic Twilight. I can promise you that."

That didn't make Mystic feel better. What if she was supposed to be alone like all the other

Malone women? But she didn't say that. She'd already hurt her grandmother enough.

"I love you, Hessy."

Hester drew back and smiled. "That's the one thing I can read." She kissed her cheek. "I love you too. Now get some sleep. I have a feeling tomorrow is going to be a big day."

Or more like a horrible day.

But Mystic didn't voice her thoughts before she headed to her room.

She had always loved her bedroom. The big windows let in the morning sun and midnight moon. They looked out on the backyard and the open fields beyond. Climbing roses grew on a trellis just outside the windows. In the spring, the scent filled her room.

There were no roses growing this time of year. The smells that drifted in the open window foretold the coming of fall—fresh-cut hay, ripe apples, and the last flowers of summer. She stood there breathing in the scent and trying to calm her rioting emotions.

Leave Cursed? At one time, she had wanted to. But that was before she'd started her own salon. She knew Hester was right and a job shouldn't be her life. And yet, it had become that. It was how she defined herself. If she let it go, who would she be?

"Been keeping secrets, Missy?"

The deeply spoken words caused her to jump. She turned to find Buck sitting in the wicker chair in the corner. It wasn't the first time he'd been in her room. But it was the first time since they'd been teenagers. The sight of him sitting there in the shadows made her realize that her salon wasn't the only thing she'd miss. She'd miss Buck. She'd miss his eyes lighting up when he saw her. And his teasing smile and his bear hugs that almost cracked her ribs. And she'd miss the first Wednesday of every month. The one day when she could let down her guard and show her love.

She pushed the thought away. "How did you get in here?"

"I climbed the trellis." It was something he'd done often when they were teens. He'd tap on her window and she'd open it to find him grinning his lopsided, one-dimpled grin.

He wasn't grinning tonight. His lips were pressed in a thin line and she didn't need to be a psychic to know he was angry. Or to know why. She had been so busy worrying about how the news would affect the way the townsfolk viewed her that she hadn't even thought about how it would affect her relationship with Buck.

"So is it true?" he asked. "Are you some kind of love psychic?"

"I'm not a love psychic."

"Then why is there a line of people waiting outside for you to give them advice on love?"

She wanted to continue denying the truth, but her days of pretending that she didn't have the Malone curse were over. "Because they found out that I can read people's emotions."

He sat up and switched on the lamp on her nightstand. In the warm glow of light she could see the hurt in his eyes. "So you do have a psychic power."

She turned away from his hurt eyes and stared out the window. "Yes."

There was a long stretch of silence before he spoke. "How does it work?"

"I don't know how. All I know is that I can see this aura around people who have strong feelings for someone."

"What kind of feelings?"

A lump formed in her throat. She swallowed hard, but it refused to move. "Love."

Again there was silence. She tried to fill it. "I'm sorry. I should've told you. I just didn't want anyone to know I was a freak just like the rest of my family."

He snorted. "Anyone? Funny, but I didn't think I was just anyone, Mystic. I thought we were friends. I thought we were best friends. And if you didn't want anyone to know, why did you tell Delaney?"

She continued to look out the window. The almost-full moon had risen. It hung like a glowing silver egg in the night sky. "I felt like I had to. I couldn't let her get married to a man who didn't love her. I didn't realize her and Shane's engagement was fake. Or that Shane would end up falling in love with her."

"So you can't predict future emotions?"

She shook her head. "Just present."

"When?" he asked. "When did this ability start?"

She lied. "A few years ago."

Silence ensued. It terrified her. Buck had never been the silent type. He was a talker and preferred to talk things out rather than leave them unspoken. His silence made her realize how upset he was. But she didn't realize the degree until he grabbed her arm and spun her around to face him.

"You're lying," he snapped. "When did it start, Mystic?" He shook her. "When?" She had never seen an aura of love around him when he looked at her. But she had always known that he loved her by the softness in his eyes. There was no softness now. His blue eyes glittered in the moonlight like sapphires touched with white flames. When she didn't answer, he released her with a harsh snort. "Then don't tell me. It's not that hard to figure out. You got your sight when we were sixteen. That's when things changed between us."

Tears welled in her eyes, and she looked away from his icy gaze. "Don't do this, Buck. Please don't do this."

"Do what, Missy? Be honest?" He laughed, but there was no humor in it. "We took a pact to never lie to each other. But you broke that pact. You haven't been honest with me and I haven't been honest with myself. I convinced myself that nothing had changed between us, but that's not true."

Fear seized her heart in a tight grip. "What do you mean? Nothing has changed. Just because I have the sight doesn't mean we can't be friends."

"Your sight has nothing to do with it. Do you actually think I'd see you as a freak, Miss? Do you actually think I would judge you for something you can't help? What I've lied to myself about has nothing to do with your gift. It has to do with believing I could actually hang on to something that was no longer there."

His eyes still held anger, but they also held a sad resignation. "We aren't friends, Missy. Friends don't keep secrets from each other. They don't make up excuses to keep from being together. They don't avoid each other's gazes." He smiled sadly. "I get it now. When we were sixteen, you figured out that our feelings didn't match up. Instead of having enough guts to tell me how you felt, you froze me out."

She stared at him as humiliation consumed her. He knew. All these years she'd tried to keep her love for him a secret and now he had figured it out. She wanted to crawl beneath her bed and never come out. But she knew her time of hiding was over. She had to face the truth. Not just of her curse, but also of her love.

"And would it have made a difference if I'd told you how I felt?" she asked.

He studied her for a long moment before he shook his head. "No. People can't help how they feel. But at least it would've ended there. At least, this farce wouldn't still be going on. And I wouldn't still be pathetically hanging on to a friendship that isn't working for either one of us."

The pain in her heart grew. "Are you saying we can't be friends?"

"I'm saying we're not friends. We stopped being that a long time ago." He moved her away from the window and opened it farther so he could climb out.

When he disappeared, she moved closer and looked out, watching as he agilely descended the trellis and jumped to the ground. She knew she should let him go. There was nothing left to say. But she couldn't stop herself from calling his name.

"Bu-uck!"

He glanced up, his endearing features cast in moonlight.

"I'm sorry," she said as tears filled her eyes. "I'm so sorry."

For the longest time, he just stood there staring at her.

Then two words drifted up on the night breeze.

"Goodbye, Missy."

Chapter Six

"Since the hay harvesting and baling started in the south pasture, I figured I'd move half the herd over to the crop residues next week. Then when the harvesting is finished, we can move the other half."

Buck scrolled through the events he'd put on his calendar and continued to read them off to Stetson, who sat behind his desk. "I figure we'll vaccinate the calves early November. And I scheduled this year's foals for their vet check and vaccinations the following week."

He scrolled back up to make sure he hadn't missed something. "Oh, and Shane came up with new software to help me schedule the horse breeding. I asked Shane to do a workshop on it for all of us—except for Gage because he's on daddy duty—next week. If you tell me when Lily's obstetrician appointment is I'll make sure Shane schedules it around that."

When Stetson didn't say anything, Buck glanced up from his phone. Stetson was sitting back in his chair with his hands steepled against his chin studying Buck.

"If you don't know, I can ask Lily," Buck said.

Stetson lowered his hands. "It's Tuesday at nine."

Buck put it into his calendar. "Got it. I'll email everyone the time Shane and I decide on—but it won't be Thursday in the afternoon because that's Gretchen's obstetrician appointment."

He waited for Stetson to weigh in, but his big brother continued to remain silent and stare at him.

"Is something wrong, Stet?" he asked. "Because if you'd rather vaccinate the calves at the end of October that's fine with me. But that's cutting it close to cattle shipping day."

Stetson lowered his hands and shook his head. "No. The first week of November is good. I'm just a little surprised that you've planned out the next few months." He glanced at the phone in Buck's hands. "Schedules have never been your thing. And I can't remember the last time you wanted to meet with me to discuss ranch business. You usually wait for me to call you into my office to tell you what needs to be done."

It was the truth. Buck had always allowed Stetson to be in charge and run the ranch the way he saw fit. Buck was happy taking orders and doing what he was told and spending the rest of the time having fun and not worrying about the ranch.

But lately fun had eluded him. Playing poker in the bunkhouse had lost its appeal. Just the thought of riding horses and fishing made him sad. And going into town pissed him off. The only thing left was ranch work.

Working hard wasn't fun, but it kept his mind off things he didn't want to think about.

He slipped his phone back into his pocket. "Maybe I just figured out that it was time to grow up and start doing my fair share. Especially when all my siblings have other things that need their attention. Like babies and new spouses."

Stetson's eyes softened. "I know it must be hard, Buck. You were the one who always wanted to get married."

At one time that was all he wanted. But not anymore. Hessy was right. Love wasn't something you could catch by chasing after it. It was the Golden Snitch in Harry Potter's game of Quidditch. The more you chased it, the more elusive it became.

He was tired of running after something that didn't want to be caught.

He shrugged. "If it happens, it happens. In the meantime, I'm the only single Kingman left. So I should take on the lion's share of the work. And speaking of work. I better go set up a time with Shane for the workshop." He got to his feet, but Stetson stopped him.

"Before you leave, there's something else I wanted to discuss."

Buck sat back down. "Shoot."

"It's about Mystic."

This was the one topic Buck had no desire to discuss. He didn't want to talk about Mystic. He didn't even want to think about her. She had betrayed him. She had acted like she didn't have any psychic powers when she had the worst kind of psychic powers. Ones where she could slip into a person's head and read their emotions without their consent.

And she hadn't told him. She hadn't told him that she was privy to his deepest, darkest secrets. Even now, his face flamed with humiliation and anger at being so betrayed by a person he thought was his friend.

"I don't want to talk about Mystic," he said in a snappish voice he'd never used in his life with his oldest brother.

Stetson's eyebrows lifted. "Did something happen between you two?"

"No," he lied. "Nothing happened. I just have a ranch to run. I don't have time to concern myself with Mystic."

Stetson studied him. "That's not what Adeline told me. She told me that you were pretty concerned about Mystic being upset over the birthday boxes her mother sends her every year. I was going to offer to pay my investigator to find her mother. Maybe all Mystic needs is to meet her mom so she can move on."

It was so like his big brother to take control. At one time, Buck might have been grateful and taken his brother up on the offer. But not now. Now, Mystic was no longer his business. No longer his friend. And she didn't seem to be too upset about it. If she had been, she would've tried to call him. But he hadn't heard a word from her. He was fine with that. Just fine.

"Thanks, Stet, but I don't think Mystic is interested in contacting her mother. If she was, she would've tried to find her a long time ago. Now I better go find Shane and set up that workshop."

After leaving Stetson's office, Buck headed to the stables. Shane had developed a love of horses. Which was strange since he hadn't known how to ride when he'd first come to the ranch. Now, he couldn't stay away from the stables.

Sure enough, Buck found him in the paddock working with one of the cutting horses while Delaney and Wolfe sat on the fence watching. Or Delaney wasn't watching as much as yelling instructions.

"Not like that! Lean back or you'll land on your head! And lighten up on the reins! The horse knows what to do, let him!"

Buck laughed as he rested his arms on the top rail of the fence. "Talk about lightening up. Give the guy a break, sis. He wasn't born in the saddle like we were."

"He might not have been born in the saddle, but he's got a natural ability, doesn't he?" It was easy to read the pride on Delaney's face as she watched her husband guide the horse through the cutting horse maneuvers.

Wolfe snorted. "Even if he landed on his head, you'd think he was wonderful. I've never seen a woman so besotted in my life."

"You should talk." Delaney socked Wolfe in the arm. "Now that Gretchen is pregnant, you won't let her take a step without fussing over her."

Wolfe scowled. "Little good it does me. She doesn't listen to a word I say. Yesterday, I found her sound asleep on the prep island in Nasty Jack's kitchen." He shook his head. "She doesn't need to be working such long hours, but she refuses to take time off until we find more help."

Delaney held up her hands. "Don't look at me. I don't even want to wait tables, but you've guilted me into it."

Shane moved up to the railing on the horse. "Guilted you into what?"

"Working at the bar. Wolfe is complaining again about not having enough help." Delaney looked at Wolfe. "If you can't find help, maybe you should think about selling the bar."

"I've thought about it," Wolfe said. "But it would break Uncle Jack's heart. He might not show up at the bar but a couple times a week, but he thinks of it as his legacy—something he wants to pass down to generations of Kingmans. I can't tell him I'm a rancher not a bar manager."

"I might have a solution," Shane said. "But Del has to be okay with it."

"Me?" Delaney looked confused. "If it will keep me from having to work at the bar, I'm all for it."

"Even if my solution has to do with Everly?"

Everly Grayson was a college buddy of Shane's who Delaney had been extremely jealous of. Buck couldn't blame his sister. Everly was one of the most beautiful women he'd ever seen.

"What about her?" Delaney asked.

"She just quit her job. I guess her boss thought she should do more for him than just manage his restaurant. Anyway, she's looking for a new job.

And since she has a business degree and managerial and bartending experience, I thought—" Shane cut off and shook his head. "Never mind. Dumb idea."

"Wait a second," Wolfe said. "I don't think it's a dumb idea. If Everly managed a restaurant, she'll have no trouble managing a bar." He looked at Delaney. "You aren't still jealous of her, are you, Del?"

Delaney stared at him as if he'd grown horns. "Of course I'm still jealous of her. Have you seen the woman? Any women in her right mind would be jealous of Everly. She's gorgeous."

"Not as gorgeous as you," Shane said.

Delaney rolled her eyes. "Don't blow smoke up my butt, cowboy. But I'm fine with her managing the bar." She gave Shane a stern look. "As long as my husband isn't planning on working with her."

Shane held up his hands. "I'm a computer nerd rancher. Not a barkeep." He reached over and pulled Delaney off the fence and onto his lap. "But even if we did work together, you'd have nothing to worry about. I'm a one-woman man, sugar pea." He kissed her while Wolfe and Buck glanced at each other and shook their heads.

It took some convincing for Everly to accept the job. Delaney getting on the phone and talking with her seemed to do the trick. Since Delaney walked away during the phone conversation, Buck wasn't able to hear what his sister had said. Once Shane left to unsaddle the horse and Wolfe went back to the house to tell Gretchen the news, Buck couldn't help asking Delaney what she'd said to persuade Everly.

She shrugged. "I just asked if her refusing the job had to do with not wanting to move to a small town or not wanting to watch the man she loved be happy. When she took too long to answer, I told her that she needed to pull her head out of her ass and accept that Shane was never going to love her like he loved me. And maybe witnessing that for herself was exactly what she needed to move on."

Buck stared at her. "Everly was in love with Shane? But I thought they were just friends."

"They *were* just friends to Shane. But Everly's feelings run a little deeper."

"You knew this and you still let Wolfe hire her?"

"Shane had plenty of chances to get with Everly over the years and didn't. He loves her just as a friend. Which makes me feel a little sorry for her."

Buck didn't know why his mood suddenly turned so dark. Shane and Everly's story had nothing to do with him. And yet, the thought of one person loving a person who only thought of them as a friend made him depressed as hell.

Shane came out of the stables. "I just got a call from the contractor. She's made some changes to the blueprints and wants us to stop by and okay them." Delaney and Shane were building a separate barn and horse stables for their animal refuge. "But before we head to town, we need to stop by and check on our kids."

The kids he was talking about were seven orphan pygmy goats Delaney had adopted and named after the seven dwarfs. Both Shane and Delaney spoiled the animals as if they were their children. Buck had to admit that the goats were pretty cute.

"That sounds perfect." Delaney hooked her arms around Shane's neck and gave him a long kiss that had Buck feeling even more depressed. When they finally came up for air, Delaney glanced over at him. "You want to come with us, little brother? Our contractor is pretty and single."

Buck shook his head. "No, thanks. I've got too much to do here." He looked at Shane. "How does Wednesday morning at ten sound for teaching everyone how to use the new managerial software?"

"That works for me," Shane said.

Buck took out his phone and was inputting the time in his calendar when Delaney spoke.

"You know how to use your phone calendar? You're planning a workshop? And you don't want to meet a single woman? What happened to my disorganized little brother who cared nothing about ranch work and everything about finding the perfect woman and having a passel of kids?"

Buck shrugged. "Maybe he finally woke up from his dream world."

Chapter Seven

The cold Mystic woke up with on the morning after her secret came out gave her the perfect excuse to hide out in her room beneath her favorite fuzzy blanket and pretend her life wasn't in shambles.

Hester's dream had been right. A tornado had hit Mystic head on, stripping away the respect she had worked so hard for and leaving her just another freaky Malone. A freaky Malone who had fallen for her best friend. And that best friend now knew she had fallen for him. Every time she thought about it, she wished she could disappear. It would make things so much easier.

Her grandmother seemed to realize Mystic needed time. Apart from delivering hot tea and soup, she stayed away from Mystic's room. Mystic should've used the time to come up with a plan of how to fix her life. Instead, she binge-watched reality television shows and cuddled Wish. The cat wasn't usually a cuddler, but she seemed to sense Mystic's neediness and put up with it.

But Mystic only got to use her cold to ignore the world outside her window for a few days before

Hester put a stop to it. On Tuesday morning, she walked into the room, swept up the mini blinds, and opened both windows before she turned to Mystic and crossed her arms.

"I think that's quite enough of the pity party." Without another word, she swept out of the room.

If on cue, Wish got up, gave Mystic a disdainful look, and followed behind Hester.

Realizing that her grandmother and the cat were right and it was time to stop hiding, Mystic got out of bed. She skipped yoga and meditation and spent the allotted time sitting on the floor of her shower letting the steam and hot water clear her head. She wished it could clear her mind as easily. But her mind remained jumbled.

How could she fix the mess of her life? She couldn't leave town. Her grandmother was here. Her business. But how could she stay when Buck knew she had fallen head over heels in love with him? How could she ever look him in the eyes again? How could she live in the same town with him? And how could she run a business when everyone would want her to read their love aura?

The questions kept circling around and around in her head as she got out of the shower and got dressed. Downstairs, she found Hester sitting at the table with Wish on her lap and a mug of tea in her hand. Her grandmother waited until Mystic had made a cup of coffee and sat down at the table before she spoke.

"You look like hell."

Mystic took a sip of her coffee. "Gee, thanks."

"So what are you going to do about it?"

"I don't know. Everything seems to be pointing to leaving Cursed."

"Then I guess you should leave."

She looked into her grandmother's violet eyes. "I can't leave you, Hessy."

"Of course you can."

"Bu how will you pay the bills?"

"I'll have the money from the spare room in the basement." When Mystic had the basement turned into a salon, she'd also had the contractor build a spare room and bathroom at the back. It had turned out to be a profitable idea. With no hotel in town, the room was rented out most of the year. "Maybe I'll find a hairstylist to rent the room and your salon."

Just the thought of someone else taking over her salon made Mystic sick to her stomach. But Hester was right. It would be the smart thing to do. The rental income from the spare room and salon, along with the money she made on fortune-telling, would be enough for her grandmother to survive on.

"Then I guess I'll start looking for a job today," Mystic said. "After I finish with my appointments." She'd had Hester cancel her appointments on Friday and Saturday, but she still had a full schedule for this week. She knew she would have to address the entire psychic thing with her customers, but it would be much easier to do when she was in her element.

At least that was her plan until Hester threw a wrench in it.

"You don't have any appointments."

She lowered the coffee cup she'd just lifted. "What do you mean? I know I booked at least three haircuts and a color for today."

"Not anymore." Hester lifted Wish off her lap and placed the cat on the floor. "While you were hiding in your room, all your clients called and cancelled their hair appointments for this week."

Mystic stared at her. "But why?"

"I guess the townsfolk are willing to trust a psychic with their love lives, just not their hair."

Mystic was stunned. "But I've been cutting their hair for years. How does me being a psychic change that?"

"Don't ask me. In case you haven't figured this out by now, the townsfolk's logic is anything but logical."

Anger filled Mystic. "So that's it? After all the years of trimming their split ends and dyeing their dark roots, they just cut me off?"

"Pretty much. And there's probably something else you should know." Hester got up and walked to the refrigerator where she removed a folded piece of paper from a magnet clip. "This came in the mail for you." She walked back to the table and handed it to Mystic. "With everything that's been going on, I figured I should open it in case it was bad news and I needed to cushion the blow."

"Is it bad news?"

"Well, I guess that depends on how you look at it. I would consider it a blessing. But somehow I don't think that's how you're going to see it."

Mystic opened the letter and read it. It was

from the Cursed Ladies' Auxiliary Club. They were calling for her resignation as president.

Mystic was no longer just angry. She was livid.

She crumpled the letter in her fist and jumped up from the chair. "Are you kidding me? After all the charity fundraisers I've busted my butt on, they're asking me to resign? This is such . . ." She held up her fist with the crumpled paper and struggled to find the right word. Her grandmother supplied it.

"Bullshit."

"Yes! That's exactly right. It's bullshit! I have worked hard to become a successful businesswoman and prominent leader of this community and they find out I have a psychic gift and everyone just forgets everything I've done? Well, I am not going to sit back and let this kind of hypocrisy take place without a fight. This is my hometown just as much as it is anyone else's. And just because I have a gift and can read people's emotions that's no reason to discriminate against me."

She threw the crumpled letter at the trash can, uncaring that it bounced off the edge and landed on the floor. "I will not resign! I will continue to be the best hairstylist in this county. And I certainly will not be run out of town. If the townsfolk have a problem with another witch living here, then to hell with them all!"

She grabbed her laptop off the counter and sat down at the table where she wrote a scalding email to the Ladies' Auxiliary Club telling them she had no intentions of resigning. After she fired off the email to every member, she stormed out of the kitchen and headed to the front door. When she flung it open, she found a line of people outside waiting. They startled when they saw her. They seemed even more startled when she yelled at them.

"You want a psychic love reading? Then you'll need to make an appointment for a haircut. No haircut, no psychic reading." She started to slam the door, but then pulled it back open. "And the price of haircuts has just gone up. So have your credit cards ready." She slammed the door closed, but then thought of something and reopened it. "Or cash. We'll always take cash."

After closing the door, she turned and found her grandmother standing there, smiling. "Looks like you figured out who you are and what you want."

The next week passed in a haze. Mystic had never been so busy. People from Cursed and surrounding areas clamored to get hair appointments. So much so that Hester had been forced to answer the phone in the salon while Mystic cut hair and gave love readings. Although the love readings started to dwindle when people realized Mystic wasn't a know-all love guru.

"What do you mean you can't see if I'll find love in the future?" Kitty Carson stared at Mystic's reflection in the mirror.

Mystic continued to snip at her short red hair. "Sorry, Miss Kitty. But as the sign says on the door, I don't see future love. Only present love. And there are no guarantees that even those readings will stay the same. Just because love isn't there today, doesn't mean it won't be there tomorrow. If you want a reading about the future, you'll have to talk to Hester."

Kitty snorted. "As if I would talk to that witchy woman."

"I can hear you, Gossip Girl," Hester said from where she sat behind the appointment counter reading tarot cards for Sue Ann Baker. Since Mystic's gift had come out, Hester's business was booming.

"Of course you can," Kitty yelled back. "Witches have extremely good hearing. Have you pulled out your broom yet? Your favorite holiday is just around the corner."

Hester smiled evilly. "I'll be sure to swoop by your house Halloween night."

"Could you swoop by our house too, Hester?" Otis Davenport asked. "Our grandkids are coming in for Halloween and they would love to see a witch fly by." Otis sat on the couch in the reception area next to his wife, Thelma. Thelma had an appointment for a trim and a reading of Otis's love aura. What she didn't know was that Mystic had already read her husband's aura. Every time she went into the Good Eats restaurant the Davenports owned, Mystic saw the golden aura that surrounded both Otis and Thelma when they looked at each other.

"Stop your teasing, Otis." Thelma swatted Otis's

arm before she looked at Hester. "No offense, Hester."

"None taken, Thelma." Hester continued to flip out tarot cards. "This year, I think I will dress up as a witch. But instead of flying by your house, why don't you bring the grandkids over here to go trick-or-treating?"

Mystic stopped snipping Kitty's hair and turned to her grandmother. The Malone house had never welcomed trick-or-treaters. Mostly because Halloween was one of Hester's busiest fortune-telling nights.

Noticing Mystic's shocked look, Hester shrugged. "I figure since you've started doing readings, it's time for me to retire."

Kitty seemed as shocked by the news as Mystic was. She swiveled her chair toward Hester. "Retire? But you can't do that. You're the town fortune-teller. Cursed needs you." She glanced at Mystic. "Just like we need a love psychic hairstylist—even if you can't read my love future."

Mystic didn't know who was more surprised by Kitty's comments. Her or her grandmother. Kitty had never acted like the town needed Hester. And she certainly hadn't acted like they needed Mystic.

"If you felt that way, then why did you want me to resign as president from the Ladies' Auxiliary Club?" Mystic asked.

Kitty blinked. "I never wanted you to resign from our club."

"Did someone ask you to resign?" Thelma asked.

Mystic was thoroughly confused. "I got a letter that said—"

Hester cut her off. "It doesn't matter now. That's all water under the bridge. And maybe you're right, Kitty. Maybe I'll wait for retirement. But you can spread the news that the Malone witches will be handing out candy on Halloween." She flapped a hand at Mystic. "Now finish Kitty's cut. You have a full schedule today."

The rest of the day flew by. After finishing with her last customer, Mystic went into the back room to start the load of towels while Hester headed to the house to start dinner. She had just finished turning on the washing machine when the bell over the front door jangled. She headed into the salon to find Everly Grayson standing just inside the door.

Hester had told her a week ago that she had rented out the spare room to Everly. Mystic wasn't happy about it. If Mystic had answered the phone when Everly called, she would've said the room was already rented. But Hester had made the arrangements when Mystic was hiding in her room with a cold. For some reason, her grandmother had refused to cancel them, stating something about "needing new blood in the town."

But Cursed didn't need this kind of new blood.

All Mystic saw when she looked at Everly was trouble.

Mystic had met her at Delaney and Shane's wedding and instantly disliked the woman. It wasn't just because Everly had the tall, lithe body most women would kill for—especially short women—or that she was stunningly beautiful with catlike hazel eyes and bee-stung lips. It wasn't even because of her long, multicolored hair that had obviously been color-melted in a fancy Dallas salon.

Mystic's dislike for Everly had to do with the love aura she had whenever Shane Ransom was around. Shane didn't return that love. His love aura only appeared when Delaney walked into the room. But regardless, Everly showing up in town couldn't be good for Delaney and Shane's new marriage.

Today, she wore spiked black booties, painted-on black skinny jeans, and a low-cut white tank top that displayed her cleavage and the small broken heart tattoo on her right breast. A tattoo that was no doubt connected to Shane.

"They're real."

Mystic lifted her gaze from Everly's breasts. "Excuse me?"

"My boobs. They're real." Everly glanced around. "Nice salon. A little too girlie for my tastes, but it works."

Since Mystic didn't know if she'd been complimented or insulted, she didn't reply.

Everly strutted over to Mystic's station and picked up a pair of scissors, snipping at the air. "At one time, I thought about becoming a hairstylist. But then I realized there's no money in it."

Mystic stiffened. "I get by."

"I didn't mean it as an insult. I just meant that you can't get rich off cutting hair unless you own a bunch of salons. And then you're not a hairstylist as much as a business owner."

"I'm both."

Everly set down the scissors and shrugged. "So you are. Now where is this room I rented?"

Mystic led her down the hallway to the bedroom. "The bathroom is right in there. If you need fresh towels, just let me know. I keep bottled water and soda pop in the cooler out in the salon. You're more than welcome to help yourself. And breakfast comes with your nightly rate." For friends or townsfolk's relatives, dinner did too. But Everly wasn't a friend or relative. "Breakfast is around eight."

"Eight?" Everly stared at her. "Then I'll have to pass on breakfast. That's a little too early for this gal. I'm more of a night owl. Which is why I took the job at Nasty Jack's."

"So I heard." Kitty had spread it all over town that Nasty Jack's was getting a new manager. Mystic knew it wasn't any of her business, but she couldn't help herself. Delaney was her friend and this woman was up to no good. She could feel it. "I hope you didn't come here to cause trouble for Delaney and Shane." She expected Everly to be offended. Instead she flopped down on the bed and laughed.

"I was wondering when you were going to let down the sweet little small-town girl act and get to the heart of the matter."

Mystic crossed her arms. "So answer the question. What are you doing here?"

Everly sat up. "I'm not here to break up Delaney

and Shane." She snorted. "As if I could. Those two are obnoxiously crazy about each other. I'm here because I needed a job and I owe Shane a favor."

"So you still love him."

Everly smiled sadly. "That's the funny thing about love. It refuses to listen to logic. All you can do is ignore it and hope it turns its attention to someone who can love you back."

Mystic realized she was more like Everly than she'd thought.

Chapter Eight

BUCK WAS BEAT. BUT AS he stood there looking at the rolled bales of freshly cut hay stacked to the rafters of the warehouse, he couldn't help feeling a sense of pride. He'd always helped with hay harvesting, but he'd never coordinated it and overseen it like he had this year. No wonder Stetson enjoyed being in charge. There was a feeling of accomplishment that came with being the one responsible for making sure a huge job got done.

Of course, he'd had a lot of help. If Stetson had taught him anything, he'd taught him how to appreciate the men and women who put in a hard day's work for the ranch.

He turned to the hay crew and smiled. "Great job, y'all. Tonight at Nasty Jack's the beer's on me!"

There was a chorus of whoops before Mitch stepped up. "A beer? That's all we get for working our asses off, Buck?"

Surprisingly, Wolfe hadn't fired Mitch. Probably because he'd been too busy looking for someone to help with the bar. Always wanting to give a man a chance to prove himself, Buck had kept him on. But Wolfe had been right. Mitch wasn't a good worker. Or even a good man. He'd caused more than a few fights in the bunkhouse. He took more breaks than he worked. Tab had caught him napping two more times in the stables. And he continued to be disrespectful.

"I believe everyone here is being paid well, Mitch," Buck said.

Mitch smirked. "But not as well as the filthy rich Kingmans."

Buck couldn't believe the man's audacity. It was the final straw. "You're fired. Collect your gear from the bunkhouse and leave an address where we can send your check." He turned to leave, but Mitch grabbed his arm.

"You're firing me?"

Buck's first thought was to punch Mitch right in the face. But Stetson had taught him that a good boss always keeps his cool. So he took a deep breath and released it slowly before he spoke. "Yes, I'm firing you. Now get your hand off me and get the fuck off my property."

Mitch stared at him for a long moment before he turned and walked away. When he was gone, Buck looked at the ranch hand closest to him.

"Make sure to let me know if he's not out by the time you get back to the bunkhouse, Sam."

"Yes, sir, boss," Sam said.

It was the first time anyone had ever called him boss. He realized it had a nice ring to it. He also realized that it was a title you had to earn. He still had some work to do before he would feel like he'd earned it.

After telling the crew he'd see them later at Nasty Jack's, he headed to his truck with one thought.

A long, hot shower.

But when he stepped into the mudroom of the castle, the smell of Potts's chicken enchiladas made his stomach growl in hunger. He'd eat first and then take a shower. He washed up at the mudroom sink before he headed into the kitchen. He expected to find Potts slaving away at the stove. Instead he found Adeline walking the floor with a fussing Daniel.

Buck was tired, but Adeline looked exhausted.

"Hey, Addie," he said. "Where is everyone?"

"Wolfe and Gretchen are at Nasty Jack's. I guess Everly arrived and they're training her. Delaney and Shane are having a picnic in their new barn. Stetson and Lily decided to have a quiet dinner at their cottage. Uncle Jack is playing chess in the stables with Tab. And Gage is sound asleep upstairs." She continued to pace and jostle the blanket-wrapped baby. "He had the three o'clock morning shift with Danny and is exhausted. Potts left enchiladas warming in the oven if you want some."

Buck was starving, but he figured he could wait a little longer to eat. He walked over and held out his hands. "Here, let me see that little guy."

Adeline didn't hesitate to hand Danny over before she flopped down in a chair with a sigh. "Good luck. Early mornings and evenings seem to be his fussy time. I've nursed him, changed him, and swaddled him, but nothing seems to work."

Buck held the burrito-wrapped baby out in front of him and studied his nephew. Danny had a cap of light blond hair that matched his mama's. And his Uncle Buck's. His face was all scrunched up as he fussed and his fists were punching at the tightly wrapped blanket as if trying to break out of his cocoon.

"What's the problem, Dano?" Buck swayed his arms back and forth in a cradle motion. "You unhappy? Or do you just like to occasionally raise a little hell? Well, go ahead, partner. Raise some hell. Unlike your daddy and mama who jump whenever you make a squeak, I don't mind a little hell-raising."

Buck didn't know if it was his voice or the swaying that caused Danny to stop fussing and stare back at him with dark eyes that could turn out to be his mama's blue or his daddy's hazel. Either way, he was damn cute and Buck couldn't help but grin.

"Yep, it's me. Your Uncle Buck. I don't know any lullabies, but I do know a little ditty about a long, tall Texan who rides a big white horse." He started singing the song Adeline had taught him as a kid as he continued to sway his arms back and forth. He only remembered one verse. So he sang it over and over again. Just as he was about ready to stop swaying and give his burning muscles a rest, Danny's eyes dropped closed like the slammed trunk of a car.

Buck chuckled softly as he tucked him in the crook of his arm. "He just needed my special touch."

"Obviously." Adeline smiled at her sleeping son. "If you'd like to take the three o'clock shift, you're more than welcome."

"No, thanks. I would hate to intrude on parent bonding time." He walked over to the portable crib in the corner of the kitchen and carefully placed Danny inside. Then he headed to the stove and filled two plates with Potts's enchiladas and brought them back to the table.

When he set the plate in front of Adeline, she sent him a quizzical look. "I guess Stetson and Delaney are right."

He sat down and dug into his enchiladas. "About what?"

"About you growing up."

He laughed. "Just because I brought you food I've grown up?"

"It's not that." She studied him. "There's something different about you. You haven't been my laughing, carefree little brother lately." She hesitated. "Did something happen while I've been in newborn baby mode?"

Something had happened. But he didn't want to talk about it. Or even think about it. For the last couple weeks, he'd pushed any thought of Mystic completely out of his mind. He didn't even dream about her anymore. Something he was quite thankful for.

"Maybe I just realized I needed to step up and start treating the ranch like my own," he said.

"And nothing happened to give you this epiphany?"

"Yes, something happened. All my siblings got married and started families. I figure it was my turn to take on more responsibility."

Adeline smiled. "And your siblings appreciate it." She started eating her enchiladas. As they ate, they talked about Delaney's new animal refuge and Uncle Jack's clean bill of health from the cardiologist and Adeline thinking that Potts had a crush.

Buck laughed. "Crusty old Potts has a crush? On who?"

"Kitty."

Buck stared at her. "Miss Kitty?"

Adeline nodded. "He blushes like a schoolboy every time she stops by to deliver the mail."

"Well, I'll be damned. Those two seem like an unlikely couple."

"Love doesn't just happen for likely couples. Look at me and Danny." She hesitated. "And you and Mystic. I thought for sure if anyone would fall in love it would be you two."

Buck dropped his fork and it clattered against his plate. "Mystic is the last person I'd fall in love with!"

At his loud outburst, Danny fidgeted in his crib and Adeline stared at Buck with surprise.

"I'm sorry," he said. "I just am tired of people pairing me with Mystic."

She hesitated. "Delaney mentioned you were upset over Mystic's psychic powers."

Buck snorted. "She doesn't have psychic powers."

"She was the only one who knew Delaney and Shane's engagement was fake."

"Any idiot with eyes could tell that it was lust not love that first got Shane and Del together. Mystic doesn't have some amazing psychic gift. In fact, I think her so-called powers are as fake as her grandmother's"

"But I thought you believed in Hester's powers."

"Well, I don't now." He got up and carried his plate to the sink. But he should have known Adeline wouldn't let it go. When he turned to put his plate and utensils in the dishwasher, she was standing there giving him the same calm, mothering look she used to give him when he was a kid and she wanted him to confess about something.

"What happened between you and Mystic, Buck? I don't think your anger is just about her psychic gift. Did you two get in a fight? She hasn't been to the ranch lately. Not even to see Danny. She sent him the cutest little stuffed horse and cowboy booties, but I don't understand why she didn't bring them herself. And that email she sent to all the members of the ladies' club stating she planned to continue being the president was pretty hostile. At first, I thought Kitty had asked her to resign. But when I talked to Kitty, she said that no one had even mentioned resigning to Mystic. I don't understand what's going on with you two."

He wanted to end the conversation right there,

push past his sister, and keep running from his thoughts about Mystic. But running had only made him feel more raw and angry. If he didn't want to explode, he needed to release some of his anger.

"What's going on is that Mystic lied to me. She lied to me after we made a pact that we would never lie to each other. And the Kingmans know better than most how lies can poison a relationship. I won't be like Mama. I won't ruin my life by caring for a person who can't be truthful."

Adeline placed a hand on his arm. "Oh, Buck. Mystic is nothing like our daddy. Daddy lied to hide all his affairs. I'm sure Mystic lied because she didn't want you to think less of her."

"That wasn't the reason. She lied because she didn't want me knowing she'd read all my emotions."

Adeline's gaze grew intent. "What emotions would those be, Buck?"

He sighed and ran a hand through his hair. "I've had a lot of emotions for Mystic over the years. Hell, we were teenagers together. And teenage boys' emotions are all over the place."

"Ahh." Adeline smiled. "So you do believe she has a gift and you're worried she looked into your brain and saw all your horny teenage thoughts."

That was some of it. He'd been fourteen when he'd started to take notice of the changes in Mystic's body. The way her butt filled out her jean cutoffs and the way her T-shirts hugged the soft swells of her breasts. That's when the sex dreams had started.

"You're being foolish, Buck." Adeline broke into his thoughts. "I don't think Mystic has the power to look into your brain and read all your thoughts. And even if she could read your lust, most teenage girls know teenage boys think about sex all the time. I doubt she thought anything of it." She hesitated. "Unless, your lust for her hasn't stopped."

"It's stopped." At least, it had stopped after finding out she had lied to him. "Mystic is the last person in the world I want to go to bed with. I doubt any man in town would want to go to bed with someone who can read their emotions like a friggin' book—a woman who would know if you loved her even before you knew yourself."

Adeline studied him. "And do you love her, Buck?"

"No."

"Did you?"

He didn't want to answer the question. He had never wanted to answer that question. But there had been that one night—the night they had been lying in the hayloft looking at the stars—when he'd turned to Mystic and all his lust and longing had turned into something else. Something he might have put a name to if Mystic hadn't gotten up and run away as if the hounds of hell were after her.

Now he knew why.

She had told him all the Malone women got their sight when they turned sixteen. She had just turned sixteen that night in the hayloft. After that night, everything changed. She didn't come to the ranch as much and became all wrapped up in becoming a hairstylist. Now he knew all the excuses she gave him for why they couldn't hang out were all lies. Lies to keep Buck from getting too emotionally attached.

"It was just puppy love," he said firmly.

Adeline squeezed his arm. "Then I'm sure that's why Mystic didn't tell you about her psychic gift. She didn't want to hurt you. I know all about that. I didn't tell Danny my feelings weren't the same as his because I didn't want to hurt him. But I ended up hurting him anyway."

"You're not responsible for what happened to Danny," Buck said.

"I know. But I am responsible for not being honest with him and breaking things off sooner. It's just hard to hurt a friend you've known all your life." She paused. "You can't be angry at Mystic for that, Buck. Or for not having the same feelings you do."

"Did. I don't have those feelings anymore."

Adeline smiled sadly. "Then why are you so angry?"

"Because what person wants someone knowing everything they're feeling? Feelings aren't things you have any control over. They just happen. And I don't want anyone reading them. They're my feelings." He thumped his chest. "Mine. If I want to express them, I will. If I don't, I won't. I certainly don't want some woman hopping into my head and dissecting them without my permission."

Gage walked into the room, looking like

he'd just woken up. "Everything okay? Where's Danny?"

Adeline turned to him. "He's sleeping. Buck has the magic touch."

Gage yawned widely. "I'm glad someone does. I'll take over moving the cattle tomorrow, Buck, if you babysit while Addie and I go back to bed."

"Sorry, but I promised the hay crew I'd buy them a beer at Nasty's tonight." Buck went to step around Adeline, but she stopped him.

"Don't be too hasty about breaking things off with Mystic. Give yourself some time and maybe you can be friends again."

Buck doubted it. But he didn't say that to his optimistic sister. He gave her a hug before he headed to his room to shower. Standing in the steamy heat, he finally started to relax. In fact, he felt more relaxed than he had in weeks. Obviously, talking to Adeline had helped him put things into perspective.

So what if Mystic knew he'd had a puppy love crush on her? They had been hormonal teenagers. And all teenagers had crushes. It was part of growing up. Adeline was probably right. Mystic hadn't told him about her ability to read emotions because she didn't want to hurt his feelings. He could understand that.

But just because he understood it, didn't mean he wanted to resume their friendship. He didn't want a friend who could read his thoughts. What they had was over and they both needed to accept that and move on. He wasn't mad anymore. Okay, so he was still a little mad. But he wasn't as angry as he had been. He felt like now he could see Mystic and not want to punch a wall.

And they *would* see each other. They lived in the same town. They couldn't be friends, but they could be acquaintances. The type that smiled and said "hi" and then went about their business.

That's exactly what they'd be.

Acquaintances.

Chapter Nine

"Stop bouncing your leg, Mystic Twilight. You're shaking the table and spilling my tea."

Mystic hadn't even been aware her leg was bouncing until Hester spoke. She stopped staring sightlessly out the kitchen window and glanced down at the table that *was* shaking . . . and spilling the tea out of her grandmother's mug.

She placed a hand on her knee to stop the bouncing. "Sorry. I guess I'm a little nervous about the Cursed Ladies' Auxiliary meeting tonight at Nasty Jack's."

Since the townsfolk had learned about her psychic ability, she had yet to venture out of her house. She spent her days working in the salon and her nights watching television with Hester. Just the thought of heading over to the bar made her a bundle of nerves.

"I can't see going to the meeting as being much different than seeing folks in your salon," Hester said.

It was a lot different. In her salon, Mystic controlled the situation. There were never more than a few people there at a time. Nasty Jack's, especially on a Thursday night, would be filled with townsfolk.

"Maybe I should cancel," she said.

Hester's eyes narrowed, and she set down the napkin she'd just been using to clean up the spilled tea. "You just found your power, Mystic. Please don't tell me you're going to give it up so soon."

"I didn't find my power, Hessy. I just got ticked off and refused to back down without a fight."

"That's finding your power. Don't stop fighting now. If you want to live here, you'll need to venture out in public eventually."

"I was thinking I'd start with a trip to the grocery store."

Hester shook her head. "That's the worst place to start. People always feel like they can confront you in the frozen food section. At a bar, they'll be too busy drinking and having fun to worry about getting a psychic reading. And if they do confront you, just repeat what you've been telling them at your salon. In order for you to give a love reading, they need to make a hair appointment." She shook her head. "I can't believe how much money you've raked in the last couple weeks. If I'd known how people love to get a reading while getting their hair cut, I would've gone to beauty school myself."

People did seem to love it. But Mystic didn't. She wasn't cut out to be a psychic like her grandmother. She hated giving people bad news—even if it was ultimately for their own good. She didn't mind telling couples that they both had matching love auras. She didn't even mind telling couples that she didn't see any auras at all. What she had trouble with was when one person had an aura and the other person didn't.

That scenario hit way too close to home. She refused to break someone's heart like hers had been broken. So, in those cases, she would pretend like she was having trouble reading their auras and only charged for styling their hair.

Thankfully, most of the people who came into the salon didn't even want to know about love auras. Like Kitty, they just wanted to know if love was in their future. Mystic was thankful she didn't see future love. She would hate to have to tell someone that love wasn't in their future. She knew, firsthand, how devastating the thought was.

And love wasn't in Mystic's future. How could it be? There wasn't a man alive who would want to be with a woman who could read his emotions. Buck had proven that. If she were honest with herself, he was the real reason she didn't want to go to Nasty Jack's. She didn't want to run into him. She didn't want to endure the cold shoulder she knew he would give her. She didn't want to look into his eyes and see the hurt and anger. She'd thought it was bad not seeing a love aura, but at least Buck had loved her as a friend. Now even that love was gone.

But if she continued to live in Cursed, she would have to see him eventually. It would be better to see him in a crowd of people than alone in the frozen food section.

She gathered her courage and got up from the table. "I'll be back early. The meetings only run a couple hours unless Kitty gets on a tangent." She waited for Hester to have some snide remark about Kitty. Instead, she only picked up her tea and took a sip.

"Take your time."

All the way out the door and across the street, Mystic gave herself a mental pep talk.

You got this. You have as much right to be in the bar as anyone else in town. And if someone doesn't like a psychic drinking beer with them, that's just tough.

But it turned out that Hester was right. When she stepped into Nasty's, everyone seemed to be having too much fun to pay her any attention. That, and it was standing room only and she was so short no one could see her over the shoulders of all the tall cowboys. She looked for one tall cowboy in particular and it didn't take long to spot him at the bar.

Just the sight of him had her heart whapping hard against her rib cage and her breath getting caught in her lungs. As hard as she tried to look away, she couldn't. All she could do was stand there and let the aura of her love surround her in its golden light.

Buck sat on a barstool with his cowboy hat tipped back on his head and his arms resting on the bar. He was talking, but not to the people sitting next to him. He was talking to Everly, who was bartending. Besides being beautiful, Everly knew how to bartend. She was moving at lightning speed, filling glasses with beer, pouring wine, and mixing drinks . . . and keeping a conversation up with Buck.

Then suddenly she stopped filling drink orders and grabbed the front of Buck's shirt—the same shirt Mystic had bought him for his birthday two years ago—and tugged him close so she could whisper something in his ear.

Mystic had seen Buck with women before. She had seen him talking and flirting and dancing. She'd even seen him kissing Mary Lou Thompson under the mistletoe at a town Christmas party. But she had never seen him laugh with a woman like he was laughing now. Mystic couldn't hear his unique laughter, but she could see it. His head tipped back and his eyes crinkled and his mouth opened, flashing his white, even teeth that had had braces on them for three years in middle school.

Then Everly reached out and ruffled Buck's hair.

The sight of Everly's fingers sliding through Buck's platinum locks—locks that had always been the one part of Buck Mystic laid claim to—made something snap inside of her. A red haze consumed her. She wasn't just angry at Everly for touching Buck's hair. She was angry at herself. Angry that she was standing there seething with jealousy over a man whose aura had never matched her own.

Buck didn't love her. At least, he didn't love her as anything but a friend—and now not even that. And yet, she had spent the last ten years of her life hoping that one day she'd glance over and see a golden glow around Buck's head.

But if that were going to happen, it would've happened by now. She needed to stop hiding from the truth and accept it. Just like the couples who had shown up at her salon wanting to find the perfect match. Sometimes auras didn't match up. Instead of giving those couples false hope, she should have told them the truth. Yes, it would have hurt the person who wasn't loved, but being hurt and getting over it was better than continuing to play the lovesick fool.

Which was exactly what Mystic had been doing.

She was a pathetic lovesick fool.

No longer caring about the Ladies' Auxiliary meeting, she whirled around to leave. She bumped into a cowboy, spilling his beer all over him.

"Whoa there." He held his now-dripping glass away from his wet shirt.

"I'm so sorry," Mystic said. "I didn't see you."

He laughed, probably because he was a big man and hard not to see. His cowboy hat was tugged low, leaving his eyes and half of his face in shadow. But she could see the lower half of his face. Something about it was familiar.

"Do I know you?"

He grabbed a cocktail napkin from the bar and brushed the beer off his western shirt. "I don't think so. Have you ever been to Montana?"

"Is that where you're from?"

"Born and raised."

"Then there's no way we've met. I was born

and raised right here." She took the napkin from him and brushed at a few droplets he'd missed. "So what brings you to Cursed?"

He smiled. Again she had the feeling she knew him. "I was just looking for a beer. I hadn't planned on stumbling into a beautiful woman." He held out his hand. "Hayden West."

She took his hand and shook it. "Mystic Malone."

"Mystic?" He cocked his head and continued to hold her hand. "And are you?"

She figured there was no use hedging around the truth anymore. "Yes. I'm the town's love psychic."

"A love psychic? I need to hear more about this. Can I buy you a drink? Maybe a glass of wine?"

"Mystic prefers beer."

Mystic jumped at Buck's deep voice, but she refused to let him jumble her emotions any more than he already had. She took a deep breath before she turned to him. His hair was mussed from Everly's fingers and his eyes held a glitter that said he'd had more than a few beers. She could tell by the flat line of his lips that he was still mad at her. Although most of his anger seemed to be directed at Hayden.

"Who are you?" he asked.

Mystic made the introductions. "Buck, this is Hayden West. Hayden, this is Buck Kingman."

Neither man held out his hand. She wasn't sure why Buck didn't. But Hayden didn't because he was still holding hers. She could have pulled her hand away. But for some reason, she didn't. Probably because she had just witnessed Buck flirting with Everly. Not that Buck would care one way or the other if another man held her hand.

"So you're a Kingman," Hayden said.

It was more a statement than a question. Which explained why Buck didn't answer it. "What are you doing here in Cursed?"

"Just passing through."

Buck continued to glare. "Good."

It was so unlike Buck to be rude. He was usually welcoming to strangers. Mystic would have commented on his rudeness if Kitty hadn't hurried up.

"What are you doin', Madam President? The ladies are all waiting at the table to start the meeting." Kitty glanced at the two men who were still mad-dogging each other and her eyebrows lifted. "Of course, I can see why you got delayed. Nothin' like two hot cowboys to take a woman's mind off her bid-ness." She winked at Hayden. "And just who are you, good-lookin'?"

Hayden pulled his gaze away from Buck and finally let go of Mystic's hand to take Kitty's. "Hayden West, ma'am."

Kitty blushed. "Well, it's sure nice to meet ya, Hayden. I'm Kitty Carson. You single?"

"Yes, ma'am."

Kitty looked at Mystic. "Please tell me he's my love match?"

Hayden looked taken back and Mystic couldn't help but laugh at the woman's audacity. "You're scaring Hayden, Kitty. And like I told you before, I'm not a matchmaker."

"Just a liar."

Hayden, Kitty, and Mystic turned to Buck. Hayden and Kitty seemed speechless. Mystic wasn't. She was pissed.

"Go ahead and start the meeting without me, Kitty," she said. "I'll be there in a few minutes." Without waiting for Kitty's response, she grabbed Buck's arm and tugged him out of the bar. Once they were standing outside, she turned to him. "Go ahead. Get all your anger out now because I'm not going to spend another second putting up with your rudeness."

"Oh, you don't want to spend another second putting up with my rudeness? Well, I put up with your lies for ten years!"

"You didn't even know about my psychic ability until a couple weeks ago. So how is that putting up with it?"

"Exactly! I didn't know. I walked around for years thinking that you were normal when you weren't."

Her eyes widened. "Are you calling me abnormal?"

"What would you call it when someone can read other people's emotions?"

"So now you do think I'm a freak."

He smiled smugly. "If the shoe fits."

Anger was too mild a word to express how she felt. She could barely see through the red haze that surrounded her. "Why you self-righteous . . . asshole!" When his eyes widened, she nodded her head. "Yes, sweet little Mystic cussed. Because that's exactly what you are. A self-righteous asshole. You've been running around town since graduating from college like some arrogant Prince Charming just waiting to bestow your gift of marriage on some deserving woman. But the truth is that you don't think any woman is deserving of the honor. Your list of requirements is longer than Santa Claus's Good Kid list!"

She counted off on her fingers. "They have to love horses and cows and dogs and cats and every other ranch animal. They had to be able to ride. They have to make you laugh. They have to want a lot of kids. They have to be mothering but also independent. They have to like to dance and enjoy the occasional beer."

She lowered her hand. "And the list goes on and on. While all you have to bring to the table is the Kingman name. Well, news alert, Prince Buck. The reason you haven't found a woman to marry is because your family name and charming smile just isn't enough. A woman doesn't want a prince who has a list of prerequisites for being his wife. They want a flesh-and-blood man who gives them one thing. Unconditional love!"

She whirled to go back inside, but Buck grabbed her and spun her around.

"At least I'm trying to find love. You, on the other hand, don't even look. When was the last time you've been on a date? I'll tell you. Three years ago when you went to the Fourth of July dance with Vern Sawyer. The poor guy said he couldn't even get a kiss from you."

She stared at him. "You talked to Vern about our date?" The flush of red on his cheeks was answer enough. "How dare you!"

"I only wanted to make sure he hadn't gotten out of hand with my best friend. But it turned out I didn't have anything to worry about because my best friend happens to be frigid. You can read everyone else's emotions, but you don't have any of your own."

The slap she delivered to his cheek caused his head to snap back. It seemed to surprise them both. Mystic gasped while Buck gaped in shock. Then the strangest thing happened.

He kissed her.

He pulled her into his arms and kissed her.

Over the years, Mystic had thought a lot about what their first kiss would be like. Soft and chaste. Awkward and naïve. Gentle and loving. But not once in all those fantasies had it been this hot, needy meeting of lips. There was nothing soft, or awkward, or gentle about it. It was like a lit fuse finally reaching the point of detonation. There was no way to stop the explosion.

Buck pushed her against the wall of the bar and greedily kissed her like he never wanted to stop. And she kissed him right back. He tasted of beer and a flavor she couldn't describe. It was sweet and dark and rich and addicting. She wondered how she had ever lived without it. Or how she would ever live without it again.

It was this last thought that pulled her out of her desire-drugged haze and had her opening her eyes looking for the one thing that would make this kiss right. But she didn't see a golden aura. She didn't see anything but Buck's blue eyes staring back at her.

Summoning all her strength, she shoved him away.

He stood there with his chest heaving and his eyes confused. "Missy?" The childhood nickname had tears forming in her throat and it was difficult to talk around them. But she had to if she wanted to survive.

"This was wrong, Buck. All wrong. You're right. We can't be friends. It's best if we just acknowledge that and move on."

She turned and walked away on shaky legs.

Sadly, he didn't stop her.

Chapter Ten

All wrong.

Funny, but the kiss hadn't felt all wrong. It had felt more right than any kiss Buck had ever experienced. Even days after their kiss, he couldn't stop thinking about the soft slide of Mystic's lips and the seductive brush of her tongue and the wet heat of her mouth. He had learned something shocking during the kiss. He'd learned that Mystic might not love him, but she damn well desired him.

No matter how upset he was over her betrayal, he desired her too. The dreams weren't just a fluke brought on by his libido. They'd been precursors, or maybe even warnings, of what kind of demons would be let loose if he and Mystic ever stepped over the friendship line.

The line had been crossed.

The demons were out.

And there was no way to hold them back.

Mystic had said they needed to move on. But how did you move on from the best kiss you'd ever had?

"Buck? Are you listening?"

Stetson's voice pulled Buck out of his thoughts and he realized his big brother had asked him something. All his siblings, their spouses, Uncle Jack, and Potts were sitting around the table and waiting for him to answer.

He set the forkful of eggs he'd been holding in midair down on his plate and apologized. "Sorry. What did you say, Stet?"

Stetson studied him. "What's going on, Buck? You've been a little out of it the last couple days."

"I think I know what's going on with our little brother," Wolfe said as he placed the last stack of blueberry pancakes on Gretchen's plate. He'd been filling his wife's plate with food ever since she'd told him she was pregnant. Since Wolfe loved food, him giving her the last of the pancakes showed how much he adored his wife.

"Well, don't keep us in suspense, boy," Uncle Jack snapped.

Wolfe smirked. "Buck's in love."

Buck choked on the bite of eggs he'd just taken and Delaney smacked him hard on the back and laughed. "Is that a 'yes,' little bro?"

He cleared his throat. "No. I'm absolutely not in love with Mystic Malone."

Wolfe stared at him. "Mystic? I wasn't talking about Mystic. I was talking about Everly. I saw the way you two were hitting it off the other night at Nasty's."

"You like Everly?" Delaney asked.

Buck went back to eating. "What's not to like? She's funny and smart and tells it like it is." And she couldn't read people's emotions. Maybe that was why Mystic had pushed him away. Maybe she'd seen the lust that had consumed him and it had scared her. The intensity of his feelings had certainly scared him.

"You should ask her out," Stetson said. "You've been working too much lately. You need to take some time off and have a little fun."

Stetson was right. Dating Everly was exactly what he needed to get his mind off Mystic and their kiss. "That's a good idea, Stet. Maybe I'll see if she's free this afternoon."

"You can't this afternoon!" Adeline spoke abruptly. When Buck turned to her in surprise, she smiled and softened her voice. "I mean . . . I need you to . . ."

"Take me into town to get my heart medicine from the Cursed Market pharmacy," Uncle Jack said.

Buck looked at his uncle. "Last time I offered to drive you into town, you told me to mind my own business and you were just fine driving yourself."

"Well, today I want you to drive me." He glanced at Delaney. "And you can come too."

"Why do I have to come?" Delaney asked. "There's a storm forecasted and I wanted to get the baby goats to the barn before it hits."

"The storm's not forecasted to hit until later tonight," Stetson said. "And I think the goats will fare just fine in the pasture. Animals are instinctual about storms. They'll seek shelter if they need to. Now, you two are taking Uncle Jack into town and that's final."

Since there was no way Uncle Jack could get into Frog, Buck's big monster truck, they took Delaney's. Buck sat in the back seat and let Uncle Jack sit in the front. He still wasn't sure why his uncle had wanted them both to come along. Maybe he'd just wanted the company. On the drive into town, he seemed to enjoy regaling them with stories about his younger days. Since Buck hadn't slept well for the last few days, he couldn't help nodding off.

He woke to the sound of tires hitting rumble strips. He sat up to see Delaney pulling the truck onto the shoulder.

"What's going on?" he asked. "Did we get a flat?"

"No." Delaney pulled up behind a pickup truck parked on the side of the road. "But it looks like this cowboy did." A man knelt next to the truck's back tire.

"I'll see if he needs help." Buck got out. "Y'all stay here." As he drew closer, he realized it was the same cowboy who had been talking with Mystic at Nasty Jack's the other night.

"Hayden West."

"Buck Kingman." Hayden didn't stand or even look at Buck as he continued to undo the lug nuts. It was obvious that neither one of them were thrilled about running into each other again.

"So I thought you were just passing through," Buck said.

Hayden shrugged. "I decided to stick around for a while."

There was only one place for a stranger to stay

in Cursed, and Everly was already staying in the Malones' rental room . . . unless someone had invited Hayden to stay in the spare room in the Malones' house. The thought of Hayden sleeping that close to Mystic had Buck feeling all kinds of pissed off.

"Where are you staying?"

Before he could answer, Uncle Jack and Delaney arrived.

"Well, don't just stand there gabbing, Buck. Help the man—" Uncle Jack cut off when he saw Hayden. "Who are you?"

"This is Hayden West." Buck made the introductions. "Hayden, this is my uncle, Jack Kingman, and my sister, Delaney Ransom."

Hayden got to his feet. "I'd shake your hands, but mine are pretty greasy."

"No need to worry about that." Delaney held out a hand. "I've had worse than grease on my hands."

A smile teased Hayden's mouth as he took Delaney's hand. "Nice to meet you."

Uncle Jack was more hesitant. "Where are you from, boy?"

"Billings, Montana, sir."

"And what do you do there?"

"A little rodeoing. A little cowboying. A little odd-jobbing."

Uncle Jack continued to study him. "Who's your daddy?"

"Jimmy West."

"Your mama?"

"Catherine West."

"Good Lord, Uncle Jack," Delaney interrupted. "What's up with the interrogation?"

"I'm just wonderin' what a boy from Montana is doing here in Texas," Uncle Jack said.

Buck was wondering the same thing. Especially when Hayden didn't seem to have a good reason for being there.

"Just passing through, sir. Now I better get this tire fixed."

"We'd be happy to help," Delaney said.

Hayden flashed her a smile. "Thanks, ma'am, but I can handle it."

Delaney shrugged. "Okay, well, if you need some work or a place to rest your head, stop by the Kingman Ranch. We can always use an odd-jobs man who knows how to cowboy."

When they got back to the truck, Buck voiced his concern. "What are you doing, Del? We don't need some random drifter working at the ranch."

"What are you talking about?" Delaney waved and tooted her horn at Hayden before she pulled out onto the highway. "We hire random drifters all the time to help us on the ranch. Some of them turned out to be our best ranch hands."

Buck glanced out the back window. Hayden was still standing there watching them drive away. "I just don't get a good vibe from the guy." He turned back around. "What do you think, Uncle Jack?"

It took a while for Uncle Jack to answer. "I think we'd be smart to keep a close eye on Hayden West. What better place to do it than on the ranch. For now, I think it's best if we get our errands done and get home. We don't want to be late."

"Late for what?"

"Getting my medicine. You want me to have another heart attack?"

Since Uncle Jack had to be reminded to take his medicine, Buck was more than a little confused by his uncle's sudden change of heart.

When they got to town, he couldn't help glancing over at the Malones' house. Usually there were numerous cars in the empty lot next to the house. Especially after people had found out about Mystic's psychic powers. But today, there were no cars parked in the lot. Not even Everly's. And when they got to the grocery store, the parking lot seemed to be as empty.

"What's going on?" Buck said. "Where is everyone?"

"Let's just be glad we beat the Saturday morning crowd." Uncle Jack opened his door and got out.

It took forever to get back to the ranch. After Uncle Jack got his medicine, he wanted to stop by Nasty Jack's and get something from the room above the bar where he had once lived. But when they got upstairs, he seemed to forget what he'd come to get. He took his time looking through the now-empty closet and checking out every empty drawer in the dresser.

Finally, he shrugged. "I guess my brain isn't what it used to be."

Delaney and Buck exchanged confused looks before they followed Uncle Jack back out to the truck. As they passed the gas station, Jack had

Delaney pull in so he could buy a lottery ticket. While filling out the numbers, he changed his mind and started choosing numbers all over again.

When they finally got back to the ranch and wanted to drop Uncle Jack off at the house so they could head to the stables, he flat out refused.

"Take me to the barn."

"The barn?" Delaney glanced over at him. "Why would you want to hang out in the barn?"

"Because the smell of hay and cow shit brings back fond memories. Now take me to the barn, girlie."

As soon as Delaney drove around the copse of trees, Buck figured out what had been going on. The barn doors were open wide and balloons and streamers surrounded the large sign that hung from the hayloft.

Happy Birthday, Buck and Del!

Delaney laughed. "So that's what was going on. I was beginning to think that you were getting senile, Uncle Jack."

Uncle Jack snorted. "I am senile, but I still have enough wits to trick my niece and nephew."

"But our birthday isn't for another ten days," Buck said.

"Which is why we were able to surprise you. Now quit gabbing and park."

As soon as Delaney pulled up to the barn, most of the town came flooding out of the open doors and yelled, "Surprise!"

Buck climbed out of the truck to hugs and back slaps. As Adeline was giving him a hug, he glanced over her shoulder to see Mystic talking to Otis and Thelma Davenport. She wore a flowery shirt and tight jeans tucked into the turquoise cowboy boots he'd bought her for Christmas three years ago. Why was she wearing them? And why was she here?

Of course, she would have been invited. His family thought they were still best friends. But after their kiss, he didn't think she'd come. And why was his heart suddenly beating faster and his breath suddenly struggling to fill his lungs?

Adeline drew back from the hug and cocked her head. "You okay?"

"Just surprised."

She studied him for a second before she took his hand. "Come on. Everyone has waited to eat until you and Delaney got here and I'm sure they're ready to dive into Potts's enchiladas."

For the next two hours, Buck tried to socialize with the townsfolk without searching the crowd for Mystic. It was a losing battle. His eyes had a will of their own and were drawn to jet-black curls, violet eyes, and a bowed mouth that his lips remembered all too well. While he couldn't stop looking at Mystic, she seemed to be oblivious to him. She talked and laughed with the townsfolk as if Buck wasn't even there. As if this wasn't even his party.

It ticked him off. Why come if she wasn't going to even look at him?

It wasn't until the candles on his and Delaney's cake were lit and he leaned down to blow them out that he lifted his gaze and caught Mystic's gaze on him. He wished he could look away. But instead he just stared back at her.

How many times had he blown out the candles on his birthday cakes with Mystic standing right there watching him? Every time he had known she was wishing right along with him—wishing that his wish would be granted. But this time, before he could even finish blowing out the candles, she turned and walked away.

He should let her go. She was right. They weren't friends anymore. But as soon as all the candles were out and people applauded, he headed after her.

"Buck!" Delaney said. "Where are you going? We need to cut the cake."

"You do it, Del. You've always been better with a knife."

As the townsfolk laughed, he slipped out the barn door. Figuring Mystic had headed to her car, he walked around the back of the barn to the open field where everyone had parked. He easily spotted Mystic's dark blue Honda Accord. But when he got to it, she wasn't in it. He glanced around.

The wind had picked up since the party had started and dark clouds had rolled in. It looked like the storm would hit sooner than expected. As he was watching the clouds build, Mystic came out of the stables leading a horse.

"Mystic!" he yelled.

He thought she hadn't heard him over the wind until she glanced back and sent him a defiant look before mounting the horse and taking off.

It didn't take Buck long to saddle Mutt and head after her. He knew the route she liked to ride. He caught up with her a few miles down the road. She wasn't riding fast, but when she saw him coming, she urged her mount to a full gallop across the open pasture. She was an expert rider and Buck had to push Mutt to gain on her. As soon as he came abreast of her, he released his anger.

"What in the hell do you think you're doing? A storm is coming. Get your ass back to the ranch." He had never talked to Mystic like that before, or any woman for that matter, and her eyes widened.

"Don't you dare talk to me like that, Buck Kingman," she snapped. "I'm not a little kid you can order around."

"Then stop acting like one. That's my horse you're on. If I say your riding is done, it's done. Now get back to the house."

She glared at him, the wind whipping her dark hair around her face. "Fuck you."

She whirled the horse around and took off.

Chapter Eleven

Mystic shouldn't have come to Delaney and Buck's surprise birthday party. But there was no way she could have gotten out of it without having a good excuse. How could she tell Buck's sister that she didn't want to come because she'd kissed her brother and now everything had turned weird between them?

Not that it hadn't been weird before.

But now there was this entire physical aspect to their relationship. She had always been attracted to Buck. She'd even had some pretty hot fantasies about him. But those fantasies hadn't come close to the heated reality of their kiss.

For the last couple days, it was all she could think about. The second he had shown up at the party, she had felt flushed and overheated. It had taken all her willpower to ignore him. But when he had puckered up to blow out the candles, all her willpower had evaporated and all she could think about was how those lips had felt against hers. She had wanted to leave the party and go home. But she'd brought Hester and she couldn't ask her grandmother to leave before the cake was served.

So she had headed outside where she'd seen Lola eating in the paddock. A ride had seemed like just the thing to get the kiss out of her mind. She hadn't thought Buck would follow her and start bossing her around as if he thought their kiss had given him some kind of rights over her. She would head back to the ranch when she was good and ready to head back to the ranch and he could go straight to—

Buck rode up next to her and lifted her right out of the saddle and onto his lap. She struggled to get out of his arms. "What do you think you're doing?"

He held her firmly as he reined his horse in. "What I'm doing is keeping you from getting caught in a downpour. Have you even looked at the sky?"

She stopped struggling and looked up. The clouds had gotten thicker and darker and much more ominous. It was hard to admit, but Buck was right. A storm was brewing and she'd be stupid to be caught in it.

"Fine," she said. "I'll head to the house. But let me down. I can ride there by myself." Unfortunately, about then thunder cracked the skies and Lola, who had slowed when Buck pulled Mystic off her, bolted.

"Shit," Buck muttered.

Mystic felt the same way. Now that she was no longer struggling, she was extremely aware of the hard body that surrounded her. The press of strong fingers on her side. The hard bicep against her breast. The flex of thighs beneath her bottom as Buck wheeled the horse around and headed back to the ranch. They didn't even make it halfway before the skies opened and rained down needle-sharp droplets that stung when they hit.

Buck veered off the path and headed toward a copse of trees. Once they got beneath the trees, he helped Mystic down. "Get to the tree house!" he yelled above the wind that had picked up. She made a mad dash to the tree house nestled in a huge oak tree.

King Kingman had made sure the tree house he'd had built for Stetson and Adeline, his first two grandchildren, was as over the top as his castle. It had shutters, glass windows, a pitched shingled roof, and spiral stairs that wrapped round the trunk of the tree and led to a sturdy door with a horseshoe knocker.

It was a relief to step inside the cozy room . . . until Mystic saw the bed taking up most of the space. She froze in her tracks and stared at the king-sized mattress that was covered in a down comforter and multiple pillows. Until that moment, she'd forgotten all about Delaney turning the tree house into a sex lair for her and Shane.

Mystic wanted no part of being in a sex lair with Buck Kingman.

She turned to leave, but ran into Buck coming through the door. He caught her by her arms.

"What are you doing?"

"I don't think we should stay here." Especially

when the warmth of Buck's hands on her chilled arms had her body reacting like she'd shoved her finger in an electrical socket.

He glanced over her shoulder at the bed. When his gaze returned to hers, his eyes were as chilly as the air had become. "If you're worried I brought you here to seduce you, let me put your mind at ease. The other night at Nasty Jack's had more to do with beer and tequila than it had to do with desire. So you don't have to worry that I have a hard-on for you, Miss." He dropped his hands from her arms and removed his wet hat, placing it onto one of the hooks as he closed the door.

Her face heated, but it wasn't with embarrassment as much as anger at his dismissal of a kiss she couldn't stop thinking about. "That's good to know. Because I don't have a ... hard-on for you either."

A smile lifted one corner of his mouth. "You sure? Because the way you kissed me back said something else entirely. And you hadn't had one drink."

"How did you know I hadn't had one drink when you were busy flirting with Everly?"

His eyebrows lifted beneath the damp locks of his hair. "Jealous?"

She snorted. "Not hardly. If I got jealous every time you flirted with a woman, I'd be in a constant state of jealousy. You flirt with every woman in your ongoing search for the perfect wife."

"Geez, Missy, that kinda sounds like jealousy to me. Like you're upset I don't flirt with you."

"As if I'd want you to flirt with me. I want a

man who will love me for who I am. Not some cowboy gigolo who is searching for an elusive unicorn."

He leaned closer, his warm breath brushing her face as he spoke. "You're right. I have been searching for an elusive unicorn." His gaze lowered to her mouth and she couldn't seem to catch her breath. "And it's time I set my sights on a real flesh-and-blood woman." She thought he was going to kiss her. Or maybe she hoped he was going to kiss her. Instead he drove a stake through her heart. "Someone like Everly. Beautiful, honest, and lets a man tell her how he feels rather than trying to read his mind." He drew away and pulled his cellphone out of his shirt pocket, tapping away at the screen while she stood there feeling angry . . . and jealous as hell.

"Damn," he muttered. "I was hoping to call and let Stetson know where we are, but there's no service. It looks like we'll have to sit tight until the storm clears." He set his cellphone on the windowsill and jerked open the snaps of his shirt.

Mystic stared at the naked skin he exposed. "What are you doing?"

"What does it look like I'm doing?" He stripped off the wet shirt and hung it on another hook. Mystic tried not to stare at the muscles of his back, but she couldn't seem to look away from the way they bunched as he moved. "Since we both agree that the kiss was a mistake, I'm sure you'll be able to control yourself if I get out of these wet clothes."

Clothes?

"Don't you dare take off your pants, Buck Kingman."

He turned and gave her a wolfish look. "And here I thought you might want to play doctor."

"We were just kids when we played that!"

The teasing light left his eyes. "Yeah, I guess we were." He walked past her and headed over to the mattress while she tried to look anywhere but at him. When she finally did sneak a peek, he was stretched out on the bed with his jeans and boots still on and his eyes closed.

"You're taking a nap?" she asked.

Without opening his eyes, he answered. "Unless you have another idea."

Looking at his hard naked chest, her brain came up with another idea. But it was a bad one. "No."

He lifted his shoulders in a slight shrug. "Then I guess I'm taking a nap." Sure enough, only moments later, his breathing evened out. Buck had always been able to fall asleep anywhere. Today, she couldn't blame him. The tree house was cozy with the patter of rain on the roof and the swaying branches of the tree playing with the light that fell across Buck and the bed.

If Sleeping Beauty had been a guy, he would've looked like Buck Kingman—moonlight hair, long golden lashes, full lips emitting soft huffs of air. Broad shoulders, defined biceps, and a dusting of golden hair between hard pectoral muscles that rose and fell hypnotically.

If he was Sleeping Beauty, what part did she play in the fairytale? Certainly not the heroine who would awaken him with a kiss. The kiss they shared hadn't awakened anything. When she had pulled back, she hadn't seen a golden aura of love around his head. Or even lust. Which meant he was right. He'd only kissed her because he'd had too much to drink.

And yet, here she stood ogling him like some desperate virgin.

Not that she was a virgin. She had given her virginity away to a guy she'd met at hairstyling school in hopes that it would make her forget Buck. It hadn't. Probably because she'd never even given the poor guy a chance. She'd closed off that part of her and had become almost robotic in all her relationships. No wonder she hadn't found a man who would make her forget Buck. She hadn't wanted to forget him.

She had accused him of searching for an elusive unicorn, but she was no better. She had pretended like she was just fine being a businesswoman who didn't need a relationship, when beneath the pretense, she was pining away for only one man. This sleeping prince who had plenty of chances to fall in love with her, but never had. Buck saw her as a friend. And now not even that. Maybe that was for the best. Maybe their friendship was the one thing that had kept her heart tethered to Buck—had kept her hoping for something that would never happen.

She had kissed her prince and he hadn't awakened.

It was time to accept it and move on.

The first step to moving on was not acting like a frightened child. She was an adult woman who could be near Buck without doing something stupid. He seemed to be able to resist her. She could resist him.

She moved over to the bed and sat down on the mattress, careful not to wake the sleeping prince. After a few minutes of watching rain droplets race down the windowpanes, she relaxed back on the pillow. A few minutes later, her eyes slid closed.

She didn't know how long she slept before she was startled awake by a loud clattering. She opened her eyes and saw huge hailstones hitting the glass. She might have closed her eyes and gone back to sleep if a few things hadn't come to her attention: the mattress her cheek rested against was harder than a mattress should be. And beneath her ear, she could hear a steady thump.

Her eyes widened as she realized she wasn't lying on the mattress. She was lying on a chest. Buck's chest. Her head rose and fell with every breath he took. She tried to ease away, but his muscled arms encircled her. One hand rested on her back . . . and the other on her butt cheek.

She slowly lifted her head, praying he was still sleeping and she could somehow slip out of his arms without waking him. But when she glanced at his face, intense blue eyes stared back at her from beneath a fringe of golden lashes. They held her like a tractor beam as he bent his head and covered her lips with his.

The kiss wasn't as frenzied as the night at Nasty Jack's. This was a slow, leisurely scorching that seemed to take all thought and willpower away from her. She became a puppet and Buck was the puppeteer who made her dance with his lips and tongue and heated mouth.

As he kissed her, his hands wandered over her body—cupping her butt, tracing her spine, stroking her bare arms in feather-like touches. Desire flooded her body and she slid her hands into his hair and moaned into his mouth. The kissing grew restless and needy as their bodies moved against each other. His hips flexed and she could feel the ridge of his hard-on as he rubbed it against her.

Obviously, he did desire her.

But, sadly, his desire was never what she had wanted most.

She was about to push him away when the door crashed open and Hayden West came charging in.

"We need to leave. Now!"

Buck shifted Mystic off him and jumped to his feet. "What the hell are you doing here? You don't give me orders on my own ranch."

"Then stay here and die for all I care." Hayden strode across the floor and scooped Mystic up in his arms, then turned for the door.

"What the fuck!" Buck charged after them and grabbed Hayden's arm to stop him. Then suddenly he froze and glanced out the window. His eyes widened. "Shit!" He took Mystic from Hayden and headed out the door.

"What's going on?" she asked. "Put me down."

Buck didn't answer or comply. He took the steps two at a time as Hayden followed. When they reached the bottom, she saw that the hail had stopped and now there was just the whirling winds and an ominous low roar—like a jet engine gaining power.

She finally realized what was going on.

Tornado!

The wind whipped her hair and pushed against them as Buck headed to the truck parked in front. But he stopped when Hayden yelled at him.

"It's too late! We can't outrun it. We need to find low ground."

Buck turned and headed in the opposite direction. "There's a ravine on the other side of these trees!"

"Mutt!" Mystic yelled.

Buck headed toward where they'd tied Mutt, but the horse was gone. Hopefully, he had made it back to the ranch.

Once they got out into the open, the wind was even stronger. Dust and debris were flying everywhere and it took a real effort for Buck to even take a step.

"Put me down," Mystic yelled. "It will be easier." Buck listened, linking their fingers and clutching her hand almost painfully as they made their way to the ravine. Hayden took her other hand, as the roar grew louder.

She glanced over her shoulder, but it was too dusty to see anything. Then something hit her in the back of the head and she went down to her knees. Before she could regain her feet, Buck lifted her into his arms and pushed forward. She held tightly to his neck and prayed like she had never prayed before.

Somehow Buck found the ravine. He had to put

her down so they could climb into it. Once they were inside the crevice, the wind wasn't nearly as strong. But the sound was still deafening. It wasn't until they got to the bottom of the ravine that she heard the mehhing. All seven of Delaney's pygmy goats were huddled there. But Buck didn't give her time to greet the goats.

"Get between those rocks!" he yelled.

She crawled between two boulders and Buck squeezed in next to her while Hayden climbed between some rocks next to them. Then there was nothing to do but stare into Buck's eyes and wait. She could read the fear in the vibrant blue. She felt the same fear. She also felt guilt. She was the one who had gone riding in the storm. If not for her, Buck would be back at the ranch safe and sound.

"I'm sorry," she said, even though she knew Buck couldn't hear her over the loud roar. But he must've read her lips because he leaned in close and spoke into her ear.

"It's okay, Miss. It doesn't matter now."

He was right. It didn't matter. All that mattered was that everything could end right here. This last second could be all that was left to their lives. And she didn't want to waste it on apologies. There was only one thing she wanted him to know before she left this world.

She pressed her lips to his ear and spoke the words she had held in for so long. "I love you, Buck."

Chapter Twelve

BUCK WAS SO FOCUSED ON praying it took a second for Mystic's words to register. He drew back and looked into her violet eyes. Eyes that he knew so well. He had seen them filled with sadness, joy, and pain. Surprise, confusion, and desire. Now they held fear . . . and love. The love they had always held. The friendship kind of love. And it didn't matter. All that mattered was that their lives might end right here in this ravine and it was time for Buck to accept the truth.

While Mystic might love him only as a friend, he loved her as the woman he wanted to spend the rest of his life with. Mystic was his elusive unicorn. The template he'd made for a perfect wife. He had spent most his life looking for a woman with all of Mystic's traits. Strong. Kind. Hardworking. Funny. Flirty. Loyal. Honest. Yes, honest. She had lied to him about her psychic power, but like Adeline had pointed out, Mystic had only done it so she wouldn't hurt him. She cared for him. She might even desire him. But she didn't have the kind of love for him that he had for her.

If friendship was all she could offer him, he'd take it.

He'd damn well take it.

He pulled her close and whispered in her ear. "I'm sorry too, Miss. I'm so damn sorry. I shouldn't have gotten angry with you. And I certainly shouldn't have kissed you. We're friends. We'll always be friends."

He brushed a kiss to her temple. When he tasted blood, he drew back with fear clenching his heart. "You're hurt." He ran his fingers over her scalp looking for the injury. He found a large gash on the side of her head. He pulled a bandana from his back pocket and pressed it to the spot. She flinched and he realized that her eyes were dazed, the pupils too large. Her eyelids drooped and his fear grew.

"Don't go to sleep, Missy," he yelled above the tornado's roar. "You hear me? You stay with me. We made a pact, remember? We'll always be there for each other. That's what friends do."

"Friends," she muttered before she went limp.

"Mystic?" When she didn't respond, he gave her a little shake. "Dammit, Miss! Don't you leave me now. Don't you do it." When she didn't open her eyes, he pressed his face into her neck and whispered brokenly. "Don't leave me. Do you hear me? You aren't just my friend. You're my life."

But she didn't move, and there wasn't anything he could do about it. He couldn't carry her back to the ranch like he had when they were kids. Not when stepping out of the ravine would put her life in even more danger. So all he could do was lie there, hold her, and press his lips to her pulse—counting off her heartbeats and praying each one wouldn't be her last.

It seemed like it took forever for the tornado to pass, but in truth Buck had only gotten to thirty-three before he noticed that the deafening roar had stopped and just the sound of the wind whistling down the ravine was left.

"You okay?" Hayden yelled.

He started to yell back that Mystic was hurt when she lifted her head and looked at him. "Buck? Why are you holding me so tight? I can't breathe."

He had never been so relieved in his life. He loosened his hold. "Thank God."

She glanced down. "Where's your shirt?" She looked around. "And what are we doing in a ravine?"

He grew concerned again. "You don't remember going to the tree house? The tornado?"

Her gaze shot back to him. "There was a tornado?"

Before he could answer, Hayden climbed over to them. "Is she hurt?"

"Yes," Buck said. "We need to get her to a doctor."

Hayden nodded. "I'll go see if my truck is still where I left it."

When he was gone, Mystic spoke. "A doctor? I don't need a doctor."

"Yes, you do, Miss. The gash on your head is pretty deep."

She sent him a confused look before she

touched her head and winced. She drew back her hand and looked at the blood. "What happened?"

"Debris must've hit you while we were running to the ravine." He handed her his bandana. "Press this to it while I climb up and see if I can get some cell service. If Hayden can't find his truck, we'll need to call for help." He started to leave, but she grabbed his arm.

"Don't leave me, Buck."

He covered her hand with his. "I'm not going to leave you, Miss. You can't get rid of me that easily."

Her eyes turned sad. "I never wanted to get rid of you."

He squeezed her hand. "Then I guess you're stuck with me forever." He released her hand and climbed out of the ravine. He could see the twister moving away, but that didn't mean it couldn't reverse its direction and head back. It would be best if they stayed in the ravine, but he needed to get Mystic to a doctor as quickly as possible. He pulled his cellphone out of his back pocket, but there was still no service.

He was about to head back into the ravine when he saw a truck headed his way at top speed, sending mud and rocks flying. He assumed it was Hayden's until the truck got closer. Relief consumed him when he recognized Delaney's truck. It came to a skidding stop only feet away, and Delaney, Wolfe, Stetson, and Hayden all got out. His siblings surrounded him and pulled him into a group hug that had emotion welling into his eyes.

"How did you find me?" he asked.

"Hester had a vision of the tree house." Stetson drew back and his eyes held tears too. "When we saw that the tree house was destroyed, we thought ..."

"That we'd lost you for good, little brother." Wolfe hugged him tighter before he stepped back with anger in his eyes. "What the hell did you think you were doing riding off in a storm? You know better than that."

"He's right, you idiot." Delaney slugged him hard in the arm. "Why would you leave our party to hang out at the tree house?"

"I was following Mystic."

"Mystic?" Delaney glanced around. "She's with you? Hester was worried she went home? Is she okay?"

"I'm here." Mystic climbed out of the ravine with Hayden's help. In her arms, she carried Dopey, the littlest pygmy goat. The other six goats—Doc, Sleepy, Sneezy, Happy, Grumpy, and Bashful—followed behind her.

"My kids!" Delaney yelled as she hurried over to take Dopey from her.

Mystic smiled weakly and weaved on her feet. Buck wrapped an arm around her before she could fall.

"I thought I told you to stay put."

"I told her the same thing," Hayden said. "But I'm learning that Texas is filled with hardheaded women."

"Damn straight," Mystic and Delaney said at the exact same time.

Since there was limited space in Delaney's truck, Buck kept Mystic on his lap for the ride back to the ranch. Her wound had stopped bleeding, but it was obvious it still hurt. She winced every time Stetson hit a pothole.

"Watch where you're going, Stet!" Buck snapped.

"Sorry," Stetson said. "But it's not easy maneuvering around all this debris."

It was easy to see the path the tornado had taken. It left behind clumps of earth, tree branches, roots, and pieces of buildings—roof shingles, splintered shutters, and a broken door with a horseshoe knocker still attached.

Buck glanced at Hayden who sat next to him. "Thank you. If you hadn't shown up, Mystic and I probably wouldn't be here. How did you know we were there?"

"I saw the saddled horse bolting out of the trees and figured he'd lost his rider."

Buck studied Hayden. "And what were you doing on the ranch?"

Hayden shrugged. "I decided to take you up on your offer of a job."

After Hayden had saved his and Mystic's life, Buck owned him more than a job. "It's yours."

When they got to the ranch, Buck was worried about the destruction he would find. But despite some barn roof shingles and broken tree limbs, everything seemed to be intact.

"The animals?" he asked.

"The horses are fine," Stetson said. "Tab said that both Lola and Mutt made it back. We won't know until the storm passes how the cattle and goats fared. But I'm sure they're fine. If Delaney's goats knew how to seek shelter, I'm sure the other animals did too."

Buck glanced behind him at the bed of the truck where Delaney was encircled with goats and smiled.

"How about the town?" Mystic asked.

"We haven't gotten any reports," Stetson said. "Most of the townsfolk were here at the ranch when the storm hit."

It turned out they were still there. When Buck and Mystic got down to the basement, they discovered it packed with people. They were all happy to see Mystic and Buck were safe. But especially his family and Mystic's grandmother. Hester had never been a woman who wore her emotions on her sleeve, but it was easy to see by the tears in her eyes that she had been terrified for Mystic's life.

"I couldn't see you. I thought you were at the house." She drew back and cradled Mystic's face. "What happened? Are you okay?"

"I'm fine, Hessy." Mystic gave her grandmother a tight squeeze. "I just got a little bump on the head."

"It's not a little bump," Buck said.

"I'll be the judge of that." Doc Walt pushed his way through the crowd.

Buck breathed a sigh of relief that the doctor was still there. Doc Walt was in his seventies, but Buck trusted him more than he did the doctors at the new county hospital. He had spent plenty of time out at the Kingman Ranch, tending to ranch hands and the Kingman siblings. He'd stitched up Mystic's chin when she had fallen down the stairs of the tree house. As soon as the doctor reached them, Buck started relaying what happened.

Doc Walt nodded as he listened and carefully examined Mystic's wound. "Bleeding is pretty normal for a head injury. So is short-term memory loss."

"You think she needs to go to a hospital for x-rays?"

"I don't need to go to the hospital, Buck," Mystic said. "I'm fine."

Doc Walt nodded. "I've dealt with my fair share of head injuries—from being bucked off a horse to being kicked by a mule. Most just need a little ice, Tylenol, and bed rest. But I'll let you know if you need x-rays after I get you cleaned up and thoroughly examined."

Adeline stepped up. "There's a guest bedroom that will be more private. And I'll get you whatever you need, Doc Walt."

Adeline guided Mystic and the doctor to the guestroom in the basement. Buck and Hester started to follow, but Doc Walt stopped them. "Let me get her cleaned up and then you can come in. I promise I'll take good care of her."

Once they were gone, Hester spoke in a voice that shook with emotion. "I saw the tornado in a dream. I should've taken it more serious. I should've warned folks."

Buck started to soothe her worries, but, surprisingly, Kitty stepped in before he could. "Now don't go blamin' yourself, Hester. You can't predict every tornado and catastrophe that comes down the pike. Why don't you come sit down while the doc examines Mystic and I'll get you a cup of tea with a shot of whiskey—or eye of newt if you prefer."

That seemed to snap Hester out of her self-blame. "I would love a little eye of newt, Gossip Girl. But since newts are hard to come by in Texas, I'll settle for the whiskey."

When they were gone, Buck paced the floor in front of the guestroom door . . . until Delaney showed up with a shirt. "I figured your shirtlessness has generated enough gossip, little brother."

Buck pulled on the T-shirt. "What kind of gossip?"

"Everyone is trying to figure out how you lost it. Some folks think it got blown off by the tornado. Some think a tree branch grabbed it and ripped it off. And there are other folks—like me—that have another theory."

"And what's that?"

"Mystic tore it off when you were in the throes of heated passion."

He would have laughed if it had been funny. But Mystic ripping off his shirt in the throes of heated passion wasn't funny. It was hot. And if he wanted to remain friends with Mystic, he needed to get those thoughts out of his head.

"Mystic didn't rip my shirt off," he said. "It got soaked in the rain and I took it off at the tree house."

Delaney lifted her eyebrows. "And just what happened at the tree house after your shirt came off? It must've been something engaging to keep you from noticing a tornado headed your way."

"Actually, we fell asleep."

Delaney looked disappointed. "That's it? I was hoping for something a little more exciting." She sighed. "I guess I've been wrong all along. If you can hang out in the tree house sex lair without things getting heated, you and Mystic must only be friends."

Buck should've left it at that. But for some reason, maybe the brush with death, he told the truth. "We kissed."

"I knew it!" Delaney punched the air.

Buck hushed her. "Would you keep it down? I don't want the entire town to know."

"Sorry." Delaney lowered her voice to a whisper, or what she considered a whisper, and grinned. "So my little brother finally figured out that he loves Mystic more than just a friend."

"Yes," he sighed.

"Wait a second. If you and Mystic figured out you love each other, then why the long face?"

"Mystic hasn't figured anything out. She still thinks of me as a friend."

Delaney snorted. "Bullshit. I've seen the way she looks at you. You don't look at your friends like they hung the stars and the moon."

"Missy looks at me like that?"

She rolled her eyes. "She kissed you in the tree house. I think that says it all. I don't go around kissing my friends."

Buck stared at his sister. "Why didn't you say something before?"

"Because every time I brought it up, you kept insisting you only thought of her as a friend and I didn't want her to get hurt. She's my friend too. Although I'm sure your inability to see what was right in front of your face has already hurt her. You've dated every woman in Cursed. Which is probably the reason she never told you how she really feels."

All Buck could do was stand there and try to unscramble the thoughts his sister's belief had scrambled. Delaney couldn't be right. She couldn't be. Mystic wasn't in love with him. Was she?

The answer came in the form of four words. *I love you, Buck.*

He had assumed the words Mystic had spoken during the tornado had been out of fear and friendship. But what if they had meant more? What if their brush with death had revealed her true feelings like it had Buck's?

What if he could have his unicorn?

Chapter Thirteen

Mystic woke with a throbbing headache. The ache grew worse when she opened her eyes to the sunlight coming in through the narrow basement window. She shifted her head to look around and winced at the sharp pain that radiated from the side of her skull.

Everything came back at once. Being caught in the rainstorm. The tree house kiss. Trying to outrun a tornado. Getting hit with something and falling to her knees. Hiding in the ravine. And the words she'd spoken to Buck right before she passed out.

She winced again, but not from the pain in her head as much as the pain in her heart.

The truth was out.

There was no keeping it from Buck anymore. Nor was there any hiding from the fact that he didn't feel the same way. He hadn't mentioned love. Only friendship. At one time friendship had been enough. But not anymore. Not after he had kissed her. Not after she had survived a tornado and realized how important life was. She wasted so many years on her infatuation with Buck. She was through wasting precious time on someone who couldn't love her the way she deserved to be loved.

"Good mornin'!"

Buck appeared in the open doorway holding a tray. If the scent of cinnamon and baked bread was any indication, it was Potts's famous French toast casserole. But the scent wasn't as yummy as the picture Buck presented. He was dressed in his favorite chambray shirt, the one he wore whenever he was nervous about something and needed confidence and comfort. The soft blue cotton turned his eyes an even deeper shade of blue and conformed to his broad shoulders and muscular chest like a well-worn couch cover. It was hard not to feel self-conscious when she probably looked like what she was . . . a woman who had survived a tornado.

She sat up and tried to smooth down her tangled hair, wincing when she touched the bandage on the side of her head.

"Easy there." Buck placed the tray on her lap before he reached behind her to adjust the pillows. It was impossible to look away from the thatch of golden hair peeking out from the opening of his shirt or ignore the scent of minty toothpaste and shampoo.

"You're using the jojoba and coconut oil shampoo I recommended?" The question popped out before she could stop it.

He drew back and his lopsided smile slid into place. "I always listen to you, Missy." He finished fluffing the pillows behind her, then picked up the two white pills lying on the tray next to the heaping plate and handed them to her, along with the glass of orange juice. "Doc left them to help with the pain."

She took the pills and glanced down at the tray. "There's enough food here to feed the entire congregation of Holy Gospel on Easter Sunday."

Buck nudged Mystic's legs over and sat down on the bed. "Or two starving tornado victims." He picked up a fork and dug into the fluffy eggs heaped next to the casserole. She had thought things would be different between them after what she had said. But either Buck hadn't heard her words of love or he'd chosen to ignore them.

Either way, it was a relief.

She picked up her fork and dove into the French toast casserole that was covered in melting pats of butter and warm maple syrup. It was delicious. Before she knew it, she'd devoured it all. She glanced at Buck, who had stopped eating and was watching her.

"Sorry. I didn't mean to be a glutton and eat it all."

He smiled. "That's okay. I'm glad you haven't lost your appetite." His gaze lowered to her mouth. "And you didn't eat it all." Before she knew what he was doing, he reached out and swiped a finger over her lips.

She felt like she had when she'd shocked herself with the exposed wires of her blow-dryer. Heat zipped through her. All she could do was sit there feeling flushed and stunned while Buck stuck his finger in his mouth and sucked. "Mmm, Potts outdid himself."

Just like that, Mystic was hungry again. Just not for food. Her gaze remained on Buck's lips and she wanted a taste like she had never wanted anything in her life. Before she could do something stupid—like dive across the tray and kiss him—he got up and lifted the tray off her lap.

He turned and she thought he was going to carry the tray back to the kitchen. She was about to thank God for the reprieve when he set the tray on the dresser and came back to sit down on the bed. His smile was gone and his expression was serious.

"I think it's time we talked." He paused, and she knew what he was going to say. She knew he was going to bring up the words she'd spoken to him during the tornado. Instead, he said something that was even more upsetting. "I love you, Missy. And not just like a friend. I love you like a man loves a woman."

The words cut into Mystic's heart like a double-edged sword. All she could do was close her eyes and try to bear the pain. Didn't he know how much she had longed to hear those words from his lips? Didn't he realize she had dreamed about this moment ever since she was sixteen?

But it wasn't a dream anymore.

It was a nightmare.

"Missy?" Buck's voice held concern. "Are you okay? Is it your head? Do you want me to call Doc Walt?"

She opened her eyes to see him leaning closer.

Too close. His beloved features were more familiar than her own. The curves of his lips. The slope of his nose. The arch of his brows. His damp hair had dried and a lock fell over his forehead in a backward *C*. But there was no golden aura encircling his head.

"I'm sorry," he said. "I should've waited to talk to you about how I feel until you're up to it. You need to rest now. We'll talk later."

She didn't want to talk later. She didn't want to talk now. She wanted to stick her head in the sand and pretend he hadn't said the words to her. And that she hadn't said them to him. But it was too late for that.

"You don't love me, Buck," she said. "I'm sure you do have feelings for me. And I have feelings for you. But we can't let a brush with death make them more than they are. Life-and-death situations can confuse emotions. And if there's nothing tangible that helps you know the difference, you can think what you're feeling is real. But take my word for it. What you're feeling isn't real. There is no love aura around you when you look at me."

He stared at her. "You don't see love when you look at me?"

She tried to keep all emotion out of her voice when she answered. "No. And I never have."

His eyes filled with confusion. "But that doesn't make any sense. I love you. I've always loved you. I just didn't realize how much until I thought I was going to lose you."

"That's my point exactly. Fear confuses emotion."

"And what about the kisses we shared?"

"That was desire. Not love."

He shook his head. "You're wrong. Yes, I desire you. But I've desired other women. Not one of those women made me feel the way I feel when I kiss you. Because I didn't love them. I love you, Missy."

It took all her strength not to crumble at his words. But she had to stay strong. For both of their future happiness.

"No, you don't, Buck. You believe that you love me, but it's not the kind of love you think it is. You love me as a friend. A lifelong friend. Just like Adeline loved Danny. And look what happened when she got those friendship feelings and love mixed up."

"I'm not Adeline. My feelings aren't mixed up."

"And I know for a fact that they are."

He jumped to his feet, his eyes snapping with anger. "You know for a fact? There's nothing factual about psychic powers, Miss. You said so yourself. And now suddenly it's some kind of tried and true scientific way of discovering whether or not I love you. Well, that's bullshit!" He released a snort of laughter. "And here I was so worried you'd read my true feelings and felt sorry for me because you didn't feel the same way. But you're not a love psychic. You're just a fraud."

Her anger flared at the word. "A fraud? I am not a fraud! I can see people's love auras. You just don't happen to have one. At least not with me.

You need to accept that. And so do I. We also need to accept that our close relationship has only kept both of us from finding someone we *can* fall in love with."

"So now you don't even want to be friends?"

Unable to look into his eyes a second more, she stared down at her folded hands. "I think it's for the best."

"And I think you don't know what's best for anyone. You certainly don't know what's best for me. Look at me, Mystic." When she looked at him, his eyes were filled with anger and sadness, a sadness that had tears welling in her eyes. "You say you don't see some mystic halo around me so you don't believe I love you. Well, love isn't something you see, Missy. It's something you feel. I know what I feel. And speaking of feeling, what about you telling me that you love me? Or don't you remember saying those words during the tornado? And don't you dare give me that hogwash that near-death experiences can confuse emotion. Fear is like alcohol. It cuts through the bullshit and straight to the truth. You love me, Missy. You damn well love me. You're just too scared to admit it. And you're using your damn psychic powers as an excuse."

He turned and strode out of the room.

When he was gone, Mystic fell back against the pillows and clutched her stomach. She didn't know if it was eating too fast, her head injury, or her conversation with Buck, but she suddenly felt like she wanted to throw up. It took several deep breaths to finally settle her stomach.

"Are you okay, Mystic Twilight?" Her grandmother stood in the doorway. One look at Mystic's face and she sighed. "So you're not okay. I'm going to assume it has something to do with Buck. He looked pretty upset when he passed me on the stairs."

Mystic wanted to lie, but the time for lies had passed. "He thinks he's in love with me. But I know he isn't."

Hester moved into the room. "Ahhh, I see. And I guess you told him that."

"What else was I supposed to do? Keep my mouth shut and let him continue to believe he loves me?"

"Sometimes it's best if people figure out their truths on their own."

"Well, I'm sorry, but I refuse to let Buck get hurt because I let the farce continue."

Hester cocked an eyebrow. "You sure you aren't more worried about you getting hurt and ending up like me and your mama with a man who will break your heart?" Leave it to her grandmother to cut to the quick of things.

"What if I am? Who wants their heart broken?"

Hester sighed. "No one. And it's a good thing people don't have your gift, or the human race would've died out long ago. Sometimes it's best if you don't see too much of what the future has in store for you. Sometimes it's best if you just let things play out."

"I'm not going to let things play out with Buck if that's what you're getting at. I don't want my life ruined. And I don't want his ruined either.

He wants to find true love, and I want that for him too."

"And what do you want for yourself, Mystic Twilight?"

She leaned back on the pillow and stared up at the ceiling, trying to fight back the tears. "I want to find a man who loves me as much as I love him. Is that too much to ask? But I'm starting to think Malone women are as cursed with love as they are with their gifts."

"Well, I don't agree about the gifts being a curse," Hester said. "But Malone women have had bad luck with men." She hesitated. "Although I don't think Buck is like your grandfather or your father."

No, he wasn't. That was the problem. It would be easy to let him go if he was a loser. It was much harder to let go of a good man with a kind heart. But she had to.

She pushed back the covers and got up. She felt a little dizzy, but it quickly passed.

"What are you doing?" Hester asked. "You shouldn't be out of bed."

"I'm fine. I'll rest when we get home." She searched around. "Where are my clothes?"

"I think Gretchen washed them. I'll go get them for you in a minute. But first we need to have a little talk."

There was something in her grandmother's tone that had Mystic turning to her. "What happened?"

Hester cleared her throat. "Chance called Shane this morning to let him know how the town had fared during the tornados."

Mystic grew concerned. "Is everyone okay?"

"Everyone is fine. Most people were right here." Hester hesitated. "But there was some property damage."

"Oh, no. Did anyone lose their business or home?"

Hester took a little too long to answer. "We did. The house is gone and so is your salon."

Stunned, Mystic sat down hard on the bed. She thought she had felt like throwing up before. Now it was all she could do to keep Potts's French toast down. Their home was gone? And not just their home, but her salon?

A thought struck her.

"Wish! She was in the salon when we left for Buck and Delaney's birthday party."

"She's fine. Everly found her and took her to Chance's. But she sure used one of her nine lives."

Mystic's shoulders relaxed, but she still felt stunned. Hester sat down on the bed and took her hand.

"It will be okay, Mystic Twilight. I know it will."

"Did you see something, Hessy?"

Hester shook her head. "Not a damn thing. But I figure a tornado taking our house is a sign that it's time to move on. There's nothing left for us here."

Mystic wanted to argue. But she couldn't.

Hester was right. There was nothing to stay for. Not a house. Or a business.

Or a handsome cowboy with beautiful blue eyes.

Chapter Fourteen

"It's shocking, isn't it? The house was here a day ago and now there's nothing but a hole in the ground."

Buck turned to find Chance Ransom standing there. Buck had been so depressed by what he'd found at the Malones', he hadn't heard the pastor walk up. While Buck and Delaney were fraternal twins, Chance and Shane were identical twins. They had the exact same features and coloring. Although Chance's sandy hair was shorter than Shane's and his brown eyes much sadder. With good reason. Chance's wife had been killed in a car accident just a little over a year earlier. Buck admired Chance for keeping his faith and starting over in Cursed after such a tragedy. If Mystic had died in the tornado, Buck didn't know what he'd do.

He looked back at the place where the house had once been. The foundation was still there and the walls of the basement, but everything else was gone. "Yeah, it's hard to believe there's nothing left. Or that the tornado didn't take more houses or businesses on its path through town. It looks like it just touched down, took the house, and left."

"It doesn't make sense." Chance paused. "But few things in life do. How are Hester and Mystic?"

"Hester seemed to be okay. I don't know about Mystic. I didn't talk with her after I found out. I just came straight here to see what the damage was." He'd also needed some time to get control of his anger after she refused to believe he loved her because of some stupid aura.

And yet, he hadn't thought it was so stupid when he'd been convinced she was reading his thoughts. He'd believed she could look into his heart. At one time, that had freaked him out. Now he was pissed she couldn't. He loved her. He damn well loved her. If he didn't, his heart wouldn't be breaking at the sight of all she had lost.

"She's going to be devastated," he said. "She loved her salon. She designed every part of it. While it was being built, I had to look at color swatches and wallpaper samples and fixtures until I thought I was going to go crazy. And now everything she spent so many hours picking out is gone. It's going to break her heart to see it."

"I'm sure she'll get over it. Hearts mend."

The words had both Chance and Buck turning. Everly stood there. Even though it was after noon, she wore a pair of shorty short pajama bottoms and a tank top that left little to the imagination. She was holding Wish. When the cat saw Buck, it jumped out of her arms and came over to greet him. While he knelt to give Wish a good back scratch, Chance pulled off his suit jacket and held it out to Everly. She didn't take it.

"Thanks, but I'm not cold."

"I'm not giving it to you to keep you warm. That outfit isn't decent."

She laughed. "If you're waiting for me to be decent, Preach, you're going to have a long wait." She sent him a sassy smile. "And you didn't seem to mind my pj's last night when you walked into my room uninvited."

Chance's face turned a bright red. "I was only checking on you to make sure you were comfortable."

"Sure you were."

Chance scowled. "Like I've told you before, I'm not interested in you, Miss Grayson. You were the one who came knocking on my door. Not the other way around."

Everly placed a hand on her hip. "I came knocking on your door because my other accommodations had been blown to kingdom come and I thought I'd find some hospitality and charity from the town preacher. Obviously, I was wrong."

"You're more than welcome to stay at the ranch," Buck said.

She turned to him and smiled. "Now here's a polite, hospitable cowboy. I'd love to—"

Before she could finish, Chance cut in. "You'll stay with me. Shane doesn't need you staying at the ranch and causing problems between him and his new bride."

Everly sent Chance an annoyed look. "If you

had let me finish, Preach, I would've graciously declined Buck's offer. I talked with Wolfe just a few minutes ago about the rooms over the bar and he said I can use whichever one I want. So you'll be rid of this wicked home-wrecker by this evening. And speaking of wrecked homes . . ." She looked at the hole in the ground. "I'm hoping you two gentlemen are discussing how to fix this unfortunate catastrophe."

Buck finished scratching Wish and stood. "There's only one way to fix it. They'll need to wait for the insurance adjusters to give them the money and rebuild. Unfortunately, that could take a year or longer, depending on the contractor."

Everly stared at him. "A year or longer? Are you telling me that you're a rancher and you've never organized a barn raising?"

"We've done numerous barn raisings, but we aren't talking about a barn. We're talking about a house with electricity and plumbing and permits."

"And you're telling me that the all-powerful Kingmans don't have any pull to get those permits? And there are no electricians and plumbers living in Cursed who would be more than happy to help a member of their community get back in their home?"

"Well, no, but—"

Everly waved a hand and cut him off. "No ifs, no buts, no coconuts." She looked at Chance. "And why do we have to wait on insurance money? Isn't that your job, Preach, to give money to those who need it? Well, two people in your town need it. And once the insurance money comes in, you can reimburse the church coffers." She turned her hazel eyes back on Buck. "Or the filthy rich Kingmans can just cough it up. From what I hear, Mystic is your best friend. So be a friend and quit standing around boohooing over how sad she's going to be and do something about it."

Before Buck could say a word, Everly grabbed the jacket from Chance and pulled it on. "Now I need a good cup of freshly brewed coffee. That pod coffee you keep at your house is shit." She rolled up the cuffs of the jacket and flipped up the collar before she patted Chance's cheek. "You really need a woman to take care of you in a bad way, Preach." She turned in her hot-pink sneakers and headed toward Good Eats.

When she was gone, Chance blew out his breath. "Talk about a tornado."

Buck laughed. "She's quite the whirlwind. But she had some good points. Why couldn't we do a house raising? I'd be willing to front the money for materials and labor. The permits shouldn't be an issue if we can find the original blueprints of the house that were already permitted. As far as getting contractors, electricians, and plumbers, it wouldn't hurt to get the word out and see who is willing to help."

Before Chance could reply, a mail truck zipped into the parking lot and Kitty Carson hopped out. She looked at the hole in the ground and shook her head. "It's just a cryin' shame, I tell you. Just a cryin' shame."

Chance smiled at Buck. "I think God just sent us a way to spread the word."

Kitty was completely on board with the house raising. "I'll get the word out that we need electricians, plumbers, and carpenters and see who bites. And I've called a special meeting of the Ladies' Auxiliary Club so we can take care of any clothes and toiletries that they need right now."

"That's very charitable of you, Miss Kitty," Chance said. "I know that Mystic and Hester will appreciate it.

She nodded, then leaned in. "Some folks might think that I don't like that witchy woman. But just between you and me, delivering mail can get pretty monotonous. Fighting with Hester is the highlight of my day. My route just wouldn't be the same if she wasn't sitting on a porch right here waiting to annoy the hell out of me."

Buck agreed. It wouldn't be the same driving into town and not seeing Hester sitting on her front porch. Or knowing that Mystic was busy in the basement snipping away with her scissors. "Then let's see how quickly we can get Hester back on that porch," he said.

Buck spent the rest of the afternoon at Good Eats, with Everly and Chance, making phone calls to try to find the blueprints of the house. Once he located those, he called Joe Wheeler, who was a retired contractor, to see if he could spearhead the project. Otis Davenport helped out by calling his middle son who managed a lumberyard outside of Amarillo for the building materials to get the framing started. His wife, Thelma, called a cousin who sold plumbing fixtures.

"'Ask and you shall receive in spades.'" Everly glanced over at Chance and grinned. "Did I get that right, Preach?"

Chance didn't smile, but it looked like he was having a hard time keeping from it. "Close enough."

Everly must've seen it too because she winked at Buck. "I think I'm growing on him."

"Not hardly," Chance grumbled.

About then Kitty came hurrying in the door. She didn't look happy.

"What's wrong?" Buck asked. "Didn't you find anyone to help?"

"Everyone wants to help. That's not the problem. It's that darn stubborn witch Hester Malone! I should've known she'd screw up a good plan and refuse any charity the town offered. When I stopped to deliver the mail at the Kingman Ranch, she told she doesn't want to rebuild the house because she and Mystic are moving away. Who in their right mind would want to move from Cursed?"

Buck felt like his heart had been kicked by a mule. Mystic couldn't leave Cursed. This was her home. And she was his . . . he didn't know what she was to him now. All he knew was that he didn't want her to leave.

When he got to the ranch, Adeline informed him Mystic was sleeping and Hester had gone for a walk in the garden. Not wanting to wake Mystic, he went in search of Hester. He found her in the secret garden in the center of the hedge labyrinth. She sat on the ledge of the fountain with her eyes closed and her hand holding the crystal hanging from her neck. Without opening her eyes, she spoke.

"So I guess Gossip Girl didn't waste any time blabbing."

He moved closer to the fountain and set the cat he carried down. "You can't leave, Hessy. This is your home."

She opened her eyes and smiled when Wish jumped up on the ledge of the fountain and nuzzled her arm. She pulled the cat onto her lap as she answered Buck. "Home isn't a pile of bricks and stones."

"No. It's the place where your family and friends are."

Hester smiled. "People think you're just the carefree Kingman prince, but you always were a sentimental soul."

"I thought you couldn't read me."

"I don't have to be a psychic to see that."

He sat down on the edge of the fountain. "It was Mystic's idea to leave, wasn't it?" He took off his hat and slapped it against his leg. "Dammit! I shouldn't have forced her hand. Mystic never has liked being backed into a corner. But I didn't think she'd run. I didn't think she'd leave Cursed."

"It wasn't her idea. It was mine."

Buck turned to Hester. "Yours? But why, Hessy? I thought you loved Cursed."

"I do. Which is why I had to act like I thought we should leave. After you two had your little tiff,

I figured she'd think that leaving was her only option. So I came up with the idea first. Mystic has always done just the opposite of what people want her to. Which is how I got her to stay the last time."

"The last time? Mystic planned to leave town before?"

Hester nodded. "Right after the town found out about her psychic gift. I had to do some appointment cancelling and forge a letter from the Ladies' Auxiliary Club asking her to resign to get Mystic's contrarian juices flowing." Her eyes turned sad. "But I'm afraid that this time, it won't work. There are too many things forcing her hand. Her feelings for you being the main one." She paused and her eyes grew intent. "Do you love her?"

Buck didn't hesitate to answer. "Yes. Almost losing her made me realize how much. But she refuses to believe me. She thinks because I don't have some stupid aura floating around my head, I don't know my own feelings. But I know what I feel and I love your granddaughter. You have to believe me, Hessy."

She studied him. "I do. I might not read auras, but I've always known in my heart that you love Mystic. And that she loves you."

"Then tell her, Hessy. Convince Mystic that I love her."

"The only person who can do that is you, Buck."

"But I told her and she refuses to believe me."

"Then stop telling her and start showing her.

Not with your aura, but with your actions. So far, the only thing you've shown her is how many women in town you can date."

Hester's words hit him like a hard slap. He'd been doing a lot of talking about how much he loved Mystic, but he hadn't done any showing. In fact, he'd done just the opposite. He'd been strutting around town dating every woman he could get his hands on in his search for the perfect mate. No wonder Mystic couldn't see his aura. He'd hidden it under a cocky playboy façade. Now, he expected her to fall into his arms just because he'd told her that he loved her?

"You're right. I've been an arrogant idiot. How is Mystic ever going to believe I love her when she's had to witness my pathetic bride search all these years?"

"That is a dilemma. And I wish I could help you with it. But I have no sight where Mystic is concerned." Her eyebrows lifted. "Which could explain why I've never been able to read you. Your future is too entwined with Mystic's."

Buck hoped like hell that was true, but first he had to convince her of his love. He didn't have a clue how to go about doing that. If he had been one of his sisters, he would toss a coin into the fountain and wish to go back in time and redo all the mistakes he had made. Of course, with his luck, he'd still be a stupid kid and make the same mistakes. What he needed was to go back in time and do all the things they used to do, but do them as the man who loved her. Not as the awkward boy who didn't know how to be anything but her friend.

He paused as a thought struck him.

Maybe he could go back.

Not in time, but in memories.

Chapter Fifteen

After finding out about her home and her salon being swept away, Mystic spent the rest of the day sleeping. Part of it had to do with the painkillers. The other part had to do with depression. But when she woke the following morning, she had accepted that her home and business were gone and it was time to leave Cursed. Since her grandmother was willing to go with her, there was nothing keeping her here. In fact, her leaving would help Buck to move on and find someone he could truly love.

When Potts brought her a breakfast tray, she asked for a pen and paper so she could make a list of everything she needed to get done before they left town. First on the list was finding a hotel room. She did not intend to stay at the ranch another night.

But then Doc Walt showed up and scratched that off her list.

"Traveling in a car over these bumpy country roads is the worst thing you can do when you have a concussion. You need to stay put and rest for a few days before you go gallivanting around the countryside."

"But I thought you weren't sure I had a concussion."

Doc Walt flashed the penlight he held in his hand at her eyes. "I'm sure enough. I don't think it's wise to leave the ranch just yet."

Later that morning, she voiced her disagreement with the doctor's recommendations to Hester and her grandmother snapped at her.

"You can't go against doctor's orders, Mystic Twilight. Your bruised brain doesn't need to be jostled around in a car. And since the Kingmans have made it perfectly clear we're more than welcome, I don't see why you're in such a hurry to leave. And don't give me that nonsense about Buck and you needing to move on. You two have lived in the same town all your lives, a few more days together isn't going to change anything. If the doc says you're staying put, you're staying put."

Knowing her grandmother would just worry about her if she pushed to leave the ranch, Mystic agreed to stay a couple more days. But she refused to leave her room. She might have to stay at the ranch, but she didn't have to run into Buck. Since he hadn't been to see her since their argument, he obviously felt the same way. She knew she had hurt him. But she also knew it was for his own ultimate happiness. He would get over her.

The question was would she get over him?

It would be easier if she didn't have to see him again. But later that afternoon as she was searching for hairstyling jobs online, a black ball of fur jumped on her bed and startled her.

"Wish!" She set down her phone and pulled the cat in for a tight hug. Wish endured it for only a few seconds before wiggling free.

"She isn't one for outward affection. Just like her owner."

Mystic glanced at the door to see Buck leaning on the jamb. He wore his Bass Pro Shop T-shirt that he'd gotten when he went to Dallas for a livestock auction. His hair was mussed like he'd been running his fingers through it. She thought he would still be upset with her. But if the genuine smile on his face was any indication, he wasn't.

She didn't know why that annoyed her. Maybe because she was still upset over their conversation. But Buck had always gotten over things quickly. Obviously, he had gotten over her. Which proved that his declaration was only a byproduct of their near-death experience.

"How are you feeling? You're looking less pale so I'd say you're feeling better. But you still could use a little more color in those cheeks." He set the huge tote bags he held in his hands on the dresser. "Here are some clothes and some other things that my sisters and the ladies of the Auxiliary Club thought you might need. They guessed at your size, but I figured the clothes have to fit you better than Adeline's pajamas. How many times did you have to cuff those pajama bottoms, Shorty?"

"Don't you dare call me Shorty, Buck Kingman.

I beat you up when we were seven for calling me that, and I can beat you up again."

He laughed. "There's some color in those cheeks." He flopped down in the chair in the corner and Wish jumped from the bed straight into his lap. Traitor. Although she couldn't blame Wish for enjoying the stroke of those long, tanned fingers. Mystic felt breathless just watching them slide through the cat's black fur.

"So what are your plans this afternoon?" Buck asked. "I'm training a new cutting horse and I thought you'd like to hang out at the paddock and watch my ultimate riding skills."

The last thing she wanted to do was see Buck's muscular thighs straddling a horse. "No, thank you. You don't need anyone boosting your already too large ego and Doc said I need to rest."

"Okay, then I'll stay here and keep you company."

"Thank you, but I need to take a shower." She got out of bed and picked up one of the bags from the dresser. "I guess I'll see you later."

He looked down at her cuffed pajama bottoms and grinned. "Three times. I knew it, Shor—"

She cut him off with a threatening look before she swept out of the room as regally as she could in her cuffed, baggy pajamas.

The shower felt wonderful. She wished she could wash her hair, but Doc had given strict orders to keep the bandage and wound dry. So as hard as it was, she refrained from putting her head under the hot spray. When she was done showering, she toweled off and went through the tote bag looking for a brush.

She found more than a new brush. She found new makeup and hair and skin products and deodorant and freshly laundered clothes all in her size—underwear, a bra, socks, pajamas, a pair of jeans, and multiple shirts. With the items was a pile of get-well-soon cards from the people of Cursed. As she sat on the toilet and read each one, her eyes filled with tears. She knew when she went through the other tote bag she would find more of the same.

A tap on the door startled her.

"Missy?" Buck's voice came through the door. "You okay?"

She wiped the tears from her cheeks and cleared her throat. "I'm fine. What are you doing? I thought you had some horses to train."

There was no reply.

Putting the cards back in the bag, she quickly got dressed in a soft T-shirt and jeans. After brushing her teeth and carefully brushing her hair around the bandage, she pulled open the bathroom door to find Buck sitting cross-legged on the bed setting up a board game. Wish was grooming herself next to him.

"What are you doing?"

He kept setting up the game. "I know you, Missy. You aren't the type of person who can rest. You need something to occupy your time. Otherwise, you're going to go stir crazy and do something you shouldn't. So I thought we'd play your favorite game of Life. I call dibs on the blue car so you get yellow." She was about to say she didn't want a car because she wasn't playing Life when his gaze lowered. "I see the clothes fit."

"The town shouldn't have gone to so much trouble."

His gaze lifted to hers. "That's what friends do, Miss. They lend a hand when you need it. You'd do the same. Now come on and let's play."

She hesitated. "Play what, Buck?"

He continued to set up the board game. "Life."

She shook her head. "No. I'm talking about the game you're playing with me right now. I told you it was for the best if we stayed away from each other and moved on."

He stopped and looked at her. "Moved on? Or moved away?"

She wasn't surprised he knew she was moving. Her grandmother wasn't one to keep secrets. "So Hessy told you?"

He nodded and the sadness in his eyes made her feel all weepy again. She looked away and stared at a painting on the wall of horses in a pasture. When she spoke, she tried to keep her voice steady and strong. "It makes sense, Buck. Our house is gone. My business is gone. And what you think you feel will pass when I'm gone."

"What's your timeline? And don't tell me you don't have one. Time is everything to you."

She swallowed hard. "I was thinking we'd head for Amarillo as soon as we salvage what we can from the house."

There was a long pause before he spoke. "There's nothing to salvage, Miss."

She wondered if he was talking about the house or their relationship. Maybe both. "Then I guess we can leave as soon as Doc Walt says I can travel."

She waited for him to say something. When he didn't, she glanced back at him. He was setting the cars on the board. A blue one and a yellow one. "Since I got the blue car, you can spin first."

"I'm not playing, Buck."

He looked at her. His eyes were no longer sad. They held stubbornness and determination. She knew the look. He wasn't giving up. Not without a fight. And Buck had always fought dirty.

"I get it," he said. "You're leaving. I don't want you to, but I can't stop you. So that means we only have a few days left to be together. And I want to spend it being the friends we once were. I give you my word that I won't ask for anything else. Or spout words of love you don't want to hear. I just want these last few days together. Please, Miss."

She wanted to deny him. Being together would only make her leaving harder and more painful. But she couldn't do it. Partly because she had never been able to deny Buck anything. And partly because she wanted time with him too. Time to build memories that would have to last the rest of her life.

"Okay, but I get the blue car."

A smile broke over his face. "Deal, but I get first spin."

An hour later, Mystic had won. "I'm filthy

rich!" She tossed a handful of the fake money into the air.

Buck laughed. "You might've gotten the most money, but I'm the happiest in my little log cabin with my six kids."

"You had so many kids they didn't even fit in your car. You had to force two of them in my car."

"I figured you had room with your twins, Slater and Tater."

She cringed. "Slater and Tater? I'm not calling any of my children Slater and Tater. Slater's okay, but I don't want the kids at school making fun of poor Tater."

Buck's eyes widened. "My oldest daughter, Trixie, would never let anyone make fun of Tater. She'd stand up for him just like I stood up to the kids at school who teased you about being a witch."

She remembered well. "You didn't just stand up for me. You punched poor Bradley Sipes right in the nose and almost got a whipping from your daddy."

He grinned. "The only reason I didn't was because you told Daddy that if he whipped me, he'd have to whip you too. And I didn't punch Bradley for calling you a witch. I punched him for trying to kiss you." His smile faded, and his gaze lowered to her mouth. "I guess even then I didn't want you sharing your kisses with anyone else."

She couldn't help the accelerated beat of her heart or her inability to take a deep breath. It was so annoying how easily Buck could take control of her body. And her mind. Regardless of all logic, she couldn't help conjuring up an image of Buck knocking the board, toy cars, and all the play money onto the floor and shoving her back against the pillows and kissing her.

Instead, he kept his word and broke the spell he'd cast with a friendly smile.

"I'm starving. Are you starving?" He hopped up from the bed and held out his hand. "Come on, Miss. Let's go see what we can scrounge up in the kitchen to eat before I challenge you to another game. This time, I'm going to kick your butt."

They didn't find any leftovers in the refrigerator so Buck made his signature grilled cheese. When he set a plate on the bar in front of her, she couldn't help but smile. He'd written her name on the sandwich with ketchup. She loved ketchup with her grilled cheese. Something Buck had taught her. Although he didn't use just a little on his. He dunked every bite in a puddle of ketchup that covered half his plate.

After they finished eating, they played another game of Life. Once again, he opted for the least expensive house and ended up with a car full of peg children. After putting away the game, he talked her into going out to the stables and watching him train a new cutting horse.

He *was* an ultimate horseman. In no time at all, he had the horse following his lightest commands. After an hour of watching him, she started feeling tired. He must have seen it on her face because he handed the horse off to Tab to unsaddle and walked her back to the house.

At least, that's where she thought they were headed. But instead he took her to the garden.

The Kingmans' garden looked like it belonged on an English estate. The quaint cottage Stetson and Lily lived in was surrounded by a multitude of trees and flowering plants with stone paths winding through them. She and Buck had spent many a hot summer afternoon in the hammock beneath the big oak, swaying back and forth as they talked about anything and everything. So she wasn't surprised when they reached the hammock and Buck toed off his cowboy boots and climbed in. She *was* surprised when he scooted over and patted the small space left.

Mystic shook her head. "Absolutely not."

"Oh, come on, Miss. I know you're tired. And it's not like we haven't shared the hammock before."

"When we were skinny kids. There's not room for both of us now."

"Of course there is." He reached out and pulled her into the hammock with him—or more like onto him. The only part of her body touching the hammock was the side of her hip and leg. The rest of her body was sprawled over Buck's. She struggled to get up, but it was impossible when the hammock closed around them like a cocoon. "Now isn't this comfortable?" he asked.

She started to argue the point, but then realized he was right. There was something comfortable and familiar about being in the hammock with

Buck—even though they weren't skinny kids any more.

Buck was now all muscle and virile man, but the soft parts of her body seemed to adjust to the hard parts of his. The branches of the trees swayed in the brisk autumn wind, rocking them gently to and fro. Beneath her ear, his heart sang a rhythmic lullaby that had her letting go of all her misgivings and relaxing against him.

They swayed for a few minutes before he spoke in a low voice. "What's your dream, Mystic Twilight Malone?"

It was something they'd asked each other a lot as kids when they were lying in the hammock. She answered like she had then, even though the answer made her sad. "I want to fix people's hair and make them look beautiful so they feel confidence."

"And you do."

"Not anymore."

His arms tightened. "Don't you dare give up on your dream so easily, Missy. You'll be back to styling hair in no time. I know it."

Somehow him saying it made her believe it. But she still felt sad. She would go back to styling hair, but it wouldn't be in her own salon . . . or her hometown. A hometown filled with good-hearted people who took care of their own—even if they were the town witches.

She pushed down her sadness and asked him the question. "What's your dream, Buck William Kingman?"

He answered like he had as a kid. "To get

married and have a dozen kids . . . with a set of twins named Slater and Tater."

She didn't laugh. She stared up at the blue sky peeking through the branches of the tree and closed her eyes. "I hope your dream comes true, Buck."

He didn't answer for the longest time. She was almost asleep when she heard his soft whisper. "I hope so too, Miss. I hope so too."

Chapter Sixteen

Time was running out.

Doc Walt was through helping Buck convince Mystic to stay on the ranch. The insurance money was scheduled to arrive in a few days. And Mystic had found a job at an expensive salon in Houston.

From what Buck could tell nothing had changed between them. Mystic still kept herself closed off from him. Yes, she played board games with him. She kept him company at the stables while he trained and groomed horses and mucked out stalls. She took naps on him in the garden hammock. Played hide-go-seek with him in the hedge labyrinth. Stayed up late watching movies with him in the movie room. He made her smile. He made her laugh. He made her remember all the fun times they had had together.

But he couldn't seem to make her trust him.

After over a week of trying to prove his love, he didn't know what else to do. He was hoping that rebuilding her salon and grandmother's house would do the trick. The salon was finished and the house was almost finished. The town had come together and rebuilt it in record time. The only thing left to do was painting and adding the few furnishings the townsfolk had donated until the Malones could choose their own. And Buck wanted to decorate the salon exactly like Mystic had. But he needed some help.

He thought about asking his sisters. But Adeline was busy with the baby and had started back with her online classes to become a veterinarian. And he couldn't ask Gretchen and Lily because they were both pregnant and getting ready for their new arrivals. Plus, Gretchen still worked at the bar and Lily was still writing her children's books. That left Delaney. She knew as much as Buck did about decorating. She also was carrying most of Buck's workload at the ranch while he had been busy proving his love to Mystic.

But there was one other person he could ask to help him.

One morning after he checked on the progress of the Malone house, he grabbed a couple coffees and some donuts from Good Eats and headed over to Nasty Jack's. Everly had moved out of Chance's house and was now living in one of the upstairs rooms at the bar. Buck didn't think too much about how early it was until Everly answered the door wearing shorty pajamas and an annoyed scowl.

"If you hadn't brought coffee." She sniffed. "And donuts, I'd be slamming the door in your face, hot cowboy." She stepped back and held open the door. "But since you did . . ."

Buck stepped inside the bar. "Sorry. I didn't think about the time."

She yawned widely and waved at him to follow her as she headed back up the stairs. It looked like she had taken Uncle Jack's room. One glance around and he knew he had come to the right person to help him finish decorating the salon.

The hospital-green walls had been painted a soft turquoise with a crisp white ceiling and trim. The old ranch landscapes had been replaced with framed prints of old-time cowgirls in big ten-gallon hats and bloomer riding pants. The bedding was mussed, but stylish—white sheets and a colorful Native American bedspread. Coordinating throw pillows were scattered on the floor next to the bed. Uncle Jack's old chair had even been covered in a deep turquoise throw.

"Wow," he said. "This doesn't even look like the same room."

"I should hope not. This was the most depressing room I'd ever seen in my life. I'm tackling the bathroom next." Everly took a coffee and the bag from the tray Buck held and then sat down on the bed cross-legged.

Buck set the tray on the dresser and removed his cup of coffee. "Before you do, I was wondering if you could help me out. I need someone to do all the finishing touches on Mystic's salon. I have everything ordered. I just need you to put it all together for me. I'd do it myself, but I'm kind of busy."

Everly took a sip of coffee and sighed with

satisfaction. "So I've heard. How's your courtin' goin', Froggie?"

"My courting?"

"Shane told me you were courting Mystic hot and heavy. Delaney was more blunt. I believe her exact words were, 'My little brother is chasing after Mystic like a dog in heat.'" She opened the bag, pulled out a glazed donut, and took a big bite as Buck scowled.

"Del has no room to talk. Not when she chased after Shane the same way."

"Hey, I don't think your sister was being a smart-ass. She seemed pretty excited about you getting with Mystic. According to her, you two are destined to be together."

Buck sighed and sat down in the chair. "Now all I have to do is convince Mystic of that."

She polished off the donut in a few bites and licked her fingers. "She's not falling for your cowboy charm?"

"Not at all. I thought taking her down memory lane and playing old board games, watching our favorite movies, and doing activities around the ranch that we did as kids would remind her of how important we are to each other. But so far it hasn't worked."

Everly leaned back on the pillows and sipped her coffee. "I can understand why. Just hearing about it makes me want to take a nap."

"Excuse me?"

She shrugged "Sorry, but I wouldn't want a man taking me on a trip down memory lane. That's what you do when you're too old to get up out of your La-Z-Boy recliner—you remind each other of what you had in the past. But you're a young, virile man, who I'm assuming can still get it up. Or is that the problem?"

Buck blinked. "That's not the problem."

Everly gave him a thumbs-up. "Good for you. Now why don't you prove it to Mystic. Instead of showing her what she had with you, why don't you show her what she *could* have with you—like wild, hot, turn-her-into-a-human-pretzel sex."

It was hard to reply when his mouth had dropped open. It turned out that Everly didn't need a reply. She just kept on talking.

"I get that you're trying to be a gentleman. And every woman loves a gentleman ... just not in the bedroom. In the bedroom, we want a man who knows what he wants and isn't afraid to go after it. No is still no. But I have a feeling that Mystic isn't going to tell you no."

"She already did. She said sex would only complicate things."

Everly rolled her eyes. "Oh, sweet, sweet dumb cowboy, that's not no. That was just her saying what she thought she should say to protect her heart. On a whole, women enjoy complicating things." She shrugged. "It's just our nature." She set her coffee on the nightstand and got to her feet. "Now I need to get showered and dressed if I'm going to get your love letter to Mystic finished."

"My love letter?"

"Isn't that what the salon is? Your love letter to her?"

Buck hadn't thought about it that way. But now that Everly pointed it out. "Yes."

She smiled. "Then I'll do my best to make it look exactly like it did . . . with maybe just a little Everly flare. And just so you know, I'm not working for free. I'll demand free haircuts and dyes for as long as I'm here in Cursed. Which probably isn't going to be that long."

Buck got to his feet. "You're leaving? I was hoping you'd stay. And I know a lot of other people are too."

"I doubt your sister is."

"Delaney likes you. She knows what you felt for Shane is all in the past."

Everly smiled sadly. "Of course it is." She took Buck by the shoulders and turned him toward the door. "Now go get your woman, hot cowboy. And remember sweet memories from the past are nice, but raunchy sex in the present is better."

The entire way back to the ranch, Buck thought about what Everly said. Since she seemed to be more aggressive and adventurous than Mystic—or most women—he wasn't so sure he should take her advice. But what if she was right? What if it was time to stop showing Mystic what they'd had in the past and start showing her what they could have in the present? And the future?

When he arrived at the ranch, he found Mystic in the basement bathroom bent over the sink, trying to wet her head under the faucet.

"What are you doing?"

She straightened quickly, flinging water everywhere. "Geez, Buck." She scraped the wet hair back from her face and reached for the towel on the counter. "You scared me to death."

"Sorry, but what are you doing? Did Doc Walt say it was okay to shampoo your hair?"

She wiped the water from her face. "No, but my dirty hair is driving me crazy. I'm going to be careful not to knock the scab off. Which is why I'm doing it in the sink."

"How can you be careful when you can't see where the scab is? I'll wash your hair."

"Thank you, but I wash hair for a living. I think I can manage."

He glanced down at her wet shirt. "It doesn't look like it."

"That's because you snuck up on me."

"Still, if you don't want to knock off the scab and start bleeding again, you need help." He unsnapped his shirt cuff and started rolling up his sleeve. "Now where's your shampoo?"

She stepped back. "I don't want you washing my hair, Buck."

"Why not? You've washed my hair more times than I can count. I think it's only fair I return the favor." He rolled up his other sleeve. "Now stop being stubborn, Missy, and let me help you. I wash and groom horses all the time. I figure I can wash and groom the little bit of hair on your head.

"The little bit? My hair might be short, but it's extremely thick."

"It doesn't look that thick to me. My hair is much thicker."

"It is not!"

He shrugged and tried not to smile. "Whatever you say? Since I've never felt your hair, I can't really be a judge."

She stared at him for a long moment before she gave in. "Fine. But be careful. I'm not one of your horses."

He didn't have a problem remembering that. As soon as she bent back over the sink all he could think about was how nice her butt looked in the tight jeans she wore and how much he wanted to fill his hands with those round denim-covered curves.

"Buck?"

Mystic's voice snapped him out of his fantasy and back to reality. Mystic wasn't Everly. She would no doubt slap him silly if he tried something sexual. And then stop hanging out with him. No, it was best if he continued to take things slow.

He pulled his gaze away from her butt and focused on giving her the best shampoo she'd ever had.

Her hair *was* thick. The strands slipped through his fingers like rich silk as he doused them with the running tap water. Her injury wasn't as bad as he'd thought. The gash was small and had scabbed over and there was no bump he could see or feel.

Once her hair was wet, he turned off the water and reached for the bottle of shampoo sitting on the counter. He poured the thick, pale liquid into his palm and then gently massaged it into her scalp. He knew how much he enjoyed Mystic massaging his scalp when she shampooed his hair so he took his time.

Starting at her temples, he moved his fingertips in tiny circles along her scalp. He massaged her crown and then down to the nape of her neck, then avoiding her injury, he shampooed around her ears. He repeated the loop time and time again, enjoying the sudsy slide of her hair through his fingers.

She seemed to be enjoying it too because her body relaxed more heavily against the counter and her head drooped closer to the bowl of the sink. When he noticed her legs wobbling, he moved up behind her and braced her with his legs.

He continued to work the shampoo to a dripping lather before he turned on the water and gently rinsed it, gliding his fingers through her hair to make sure he removed all the suds. Turning off the water, he grabbed the towel and carefully blotted the water from her hair.

"There." He draped the towel over her head. "You'll have to do that twisty thing you girls do. I don't have a clue how to do that." He stepped back and waited for her to straighten. When she didn't, he grew concerned.

"Mystic?" He took her arm and helped her straighten. Her wet hair fell over her forehead and he smoothed it back. "Are you okay? Did bending over so long make you dizzy?" Her pretty violet eyes did look a little dazed. The pupils were big and her breath was labored.

"Talk to me, Missy. You're scaring me. Tell me what's wrong?"

She only said three words. "Damn you, Buck."

Then she threaded her fingers through his hair and kissed him.

Chapter Seventeen

Mystic had been doing such a good job of resisting Buck. But it hadn't been easy. When he turned on the charm, there wasn't a woman alive who could resist him. But Mystic had done it. She had stopped looking at him as the man she desired and had started looking at him as the boy she had grown up with. It had helped that he seemed to want to do everything they had done as children.

If only they had continued to play at being childhood friends.

If only he hadn't volunteered to shampoo her hair.

While she had washed hundreds of heads of hair, only a few people had washed hers. Her mother and grandmother, but she'd been too young to remember, and some of her fellow students at her stylist school. And not one of them, the men included, had made her feel like Buck did. She felt soothed and cherished . . . and loved. Maybe it wasn't the same kind of love that she felt, but it didn't matter. All that mattered was that he cared for her. With each gentle stroke of his fingers, he communicated how much he cared.

When she stood and looked into his beloved blue eyes, she couldn't stop herself from releasing the love she felt for him. Even if it was all wrong.

But as soon as her lips touched his, it didn't feel wrong. It felt like she was the one lone sock in the drawer that had finally found its match. Their mouths and tongues recognized each other like they had kissed a thousand times before and slid into a slow, perfectly choreographed dance that left Mystic feeling dizzy and breathless like she had when he'd spun her around and around on the playground merry-go-round when they were kids.

She didn't remember him taking her shirt and bra off, but suddenly they were gone and her breast was cradled in the warmth of his palm. She had always worried about being too small for his large hands, but her breast seemed to fit perfectly as he gently kneaded and fondled her.

His other hand cupped her blue-jeaned butt cheek, his fingers squeezing as he lifted her to the toes of her boots and pressed her quivering center against the hard ridge beneath his fly.

They both groaned and rocked their hips to get closer. While it felt good, it wasn't nearly enough. She pulled away and reached for the fly of his jeans at the same time as he reached for hers. It was a fumble of hands and arms as they worked to free each other of clothes. Buck got her jeans down first and she gave up her quest of pushing his down when he slipped his hand inside her panties. At the first stroke of his work-calloused fingers, her head fell back and she sighed his name.

"Buck."

He bent his head and kissed his way down her throat to her breast. "Missy," he whispered before he tugged her nipple into his hot, wet mouth. Heat exploded inside her as he worked her nipple with his tongue. When he simultaneously fingered the quivering spot between her legs, her knees turned to water and she had to grab on to the vanity to keep from falling at his boots. But not even her firm grip on the counter could keep her upright when his rhythmic strokes had her cresting the peak of an amazing orgasm.

Buck caught her before she could fall and held her up as he finished off her climax with light caresses that had her shivering her satisfaction. Then he lifted her into his arms and carried her to the bed where he tugged off her boots and finished taking off her clothes.

If there was any doubt of his intentions, it was erased when he walked to the door and locked it with a resounding click that brought her back to reality. She knew now was the time to stop things before they went too far. Before someone got hurt. Like her. But then Buck turned and softly smiled. As always, his smile filled all the empty spaces she kept locked tight inside. She loved him, and just like the first Wednesday of every month, she didn't think it was too much to ask for one night in Buck's arms.

He toed off his boots and slid out of his jeans

and briefs. The sight of Buck buck-naked left her speechless. She had known he had a nice upper torso, but she hadn't seen him without his jeans since they had been in high school and had gone swimming at the pond. His legs were no longer a scrawny teen's. His thighs and calves were toned and muscled and lightly covered in golden hair. Between those manly legs jutted an even more impressive muscle.

Her eyes widened.

"Everything okay?"

Buck's words made her realize she'd been staring. Her face flushed with heat as she met his eyes. "Yes... I just didn't realize you were..." He tipped his head and lifted his eyebrows and her cheeks grew hotter.

"You didn't realize I was what? A man?" He moved closer to the bed. "Well, I'm a man, Missy. A man who wants to treat you like a woman. If you have a problem with that, you better tell me now."

She slowly shook her head, but he wouldn't let her get away with that.

"Words, Miss. I need words."

"Treat me like your woman, Buck."

His breath fell heavy from his lips like he had been holding it before he placed a knee on the mattress and covered her with his heat and hard muscle. "Only if you treat me like your man," he whispered before he kissed her.

There was a big difference between kissing when they had been clothed and kissing when they were completely naked. Now it wasn't just their lips that kissed. It was their bodies. The hard swells of his pectorals kissed her soft breasts and his lower stomach kissed the curve of her pelvis and his erection kissed the inside of her thighs. She felt totally consumed by his heated kisses.

Desire swelled and crashed like waves on a sandy beach with every brush of his skin against hers. If she could be absorbed into his skin, she would've easily disappeared. She was disappointed when he moved to her side and took the heavy press of his body away.

But her disappointment only lasted as long as it took his fingers to slip between her legs. Then she couldn't think of anything but how his touch made her weep and tumble back into oblivion. After the last tingles faded, she opened her eyes to find him watching her with a crooked smile on his face.

"What?" she asked

"You crinkle your nose up when you come."

"I do not."

His smile got bigger. "You do too." He leaned down and kissed the bridge of her nose. "It's cute as hell."

She frowned. A woman didn't want to be cute in bed. She wanted to be sexy and wicked. But she realized that she hadn't been acting very sexy and wicked. She'd been letting Buck do most of the work. Realizing this might be the only time she got to touch him the way she had dreamed about touching him, she slid her hands in his thick hair and pulled him to her waiting lips. She kissed him deeply and thoroughly, nipping his bottom lip with her teeth as she drew away.

"Then maybe we need to see what you do when you come."

With a hard shove, she pushed him to his back. He looked startled for only a second—the second it took her to take his thick length in her hand. Then his eyes turned a darker blue and grew heavy lidded as she learned the shape and feel of his desire.

She didn't have a lot of experience in what made a man burn so she let the flex of Buck's hips and his soft groans guide her. When her hand had him slick and pulsing, she went to lower her mouth. He stopped her.

"Wait, Miss. I want the first time to be in you."

He shifted and leaned over the edge of the bed to grab his jeans from the floor. As soon as he pulled the condom from the wrapper, she took it from him. Once she had it on, she pushed him back against the pillows and straddled him.

She smiled slyly. "I dibs top."

His eyes held heat and laughter as he smoothed a strand of her hair back. "Whatever you say, Missy. Whatever you say."

It took some adjusting to make them fit. With anyone else, it would have been awkward. But not with Buck. Once he was deep inside her, they both sighed and he gave her the crooked grin before he pulled her down to his waiting lips.

He took his time, giving her slow, sweet sips of

his lips and hot brushes of his tongue. There was no rush. No frenzied hurry. Their lovemaking turned out to be as comfortable as their friendship.

They continued to kiss until Buck flexed his hips and thrust, igniting a shower of sparks deep inside her. She lifted her hips and slid back down in a slow, deep stroke that had them both moaning. Time ceased to be. There was only this moment and this sizzling heat that seemed to be consuming her from the inside out. When the flames burned bright and hot, slow wasn't enough. She drew back from the kiss and started pumping faster and harder, wanting him as deep as she could get. As if reading her mind, he rolled her over and thrust hard, knocking the headboard against the wall.

But Mystic didn't care about the loud noise each rock of his hips made. All she cared about was making sure Buck didn't stop. She hooked her legs around his hips and met each thrust. When her orgasm hit, the moan of pleasure that came from deep in her chest was almost as loud as the banging headboard.

It wasn't until Buck had climaxed and they were both lying in a tangle of limp arms and legs that embarrassment set in. She covered her face with her hand.

"The entire household must've heard."

Buck pressed his face into her neck and sighed. "Probably."

She untangled herself from him and sat up. "Probably? You really think they heard me?"

He sat up and took care of the condom before

he turned back to her with a devilish grin. "You did moan pretty loudly, Miss."

"Buck Kingman!" She swatted him.

He laughed and pulled her to his chest. "I'm teasing you. They didn't hear a thing. My granddaddy made sure the walls of his castle were built thick and we're in the basement. No one heard a—"

A knock on the door cut him off. "Mystic!" Potts voice came through the door. "You okay, girlie? What was all that racket?"

Mystic's eyes widened as she stared at Buck. He wasn't at all upset about being caught. In fact, he found it amusing. His entire face crinkled up in silent laughter. She swatted him again. "It's not funny," she whispered.

"What was that?" Potts yelled. "Speak up. I'm startin' to get worried. Do I need to get Stetson to kick down the door?"

"No!" she yelled. "I'm fine, Potts. I was just . . . doing yoga and I was doing a down dog when I lost my balance and fell into the wall."

"A down what?"

"It's a yoga move. But it doesn't matter. I'm fine."

"Well, that's good. But I don't think you should be acting like a dog after a head injury." The doorknob jiggled. "Now open the door. I brought you a tuna melt for lunch."

"Thank you, Potts, but I can't open the door because I'm . . ." She scrambled around for a reason and when she couldn't think of one, she settled for the truth. "Because I'm not dressed."

There was a long silence before Potts spoke. "Then I'll leave it right here by the door." A second later, he snorted. "Naked yoga. What is this world comin' to?"

As soon as they heard the click of Potts's retreating boots, Buck released his laughter. Mystic shot him an annoyed look and started to get off the bed, but he reached out and hooked an arm around her waist, pulling her down to the mattress.

His hair was mussed and his eyes twinkled with laughter. "I'm sorry, honey. But you have to admit that it's kinda funny."

It was the first time he had used a term of endearment to address her. It made her insides feel like warm honey. All her anger slipped away and she laughed. "It was pretty funny. But now Potts thinks I do naked yoga."

"And what's wrong with naked yoga? I'm thinking it could be fun." His gaze lowered to her breasts that were pressed against his chest. "In fact, I think we should try it right now."

"Now?"

He nodded. "Yep, now. I'll be the dog." He smiled evilly. "And I'll be happy to go down."

Mystic didn't know what he was talking about until he started kissing his way down her body. Once his hot mouth and skilled tongue reached their destination, she realized he was right.

Naked yoga *was* fun.

Chapter Eighteen

"I'M NOT SURE IF I'M ready to see what the tornado did."

Buck glanced over at Mystic. She was staring out the windshield with her hands clasped tightly on her lap. Worry and fear were etched all over her delicate features. It was a huge contrast to the happy look that had been there for the last few days. He'd prided himself on putting that happy look on her face, and it was on the tip of his tongue to tell her the truth.

But he couldn't give away the surprise. If he did, the entire town of Cursed might lynch him. They had worked their asses off to make sure the house was ready. He couldn't let all their hard work not be rewarded with the surprised look on Mystic's face when she saw the culmination of all that hard work. So instead, he reached over the console and took her hand in his.

"It's going to be okay, Missy. Trust me."

She didn't say anything. But she didn't have to. Deep down, he knew she trusted him. He also knew she loved him. She had told him just that morning when he was deep inside of her. And he had told her over and over and over again in the last few days.

"Of course, it's going to be okay," Hester said from the back seat. "I see happiness."

Buck had to bite back his grin. It had been as hard to keep Hester at the ranch as it had been to keep Mystic. Thankfully, Gretchen had thought to purchase Hester some tarot cards from Amazon and Hester had been kept busy doing readings for the entire Kingman family and all the ranch hands. But especially for Potts. The cowboy cook was extremely interested in what his future would hold. And Hester was happy to oblige.

Which brought up a good point.

"I thought you couldn't see your own future, Hessy," Buck said.

"I can't. But I can see what's going on right in front of my eyes."

Buck released his smile.

He was happy.

Mystic finally trusted in his love. Everly was right. All it had taken was treating Mystic like a woman instead of a child. It turned out they were as perfectly matched in bed as they were in friendship. Mystic knew exactly what drove him wild. And if the numerous orgasms he'd given her were any indication, he knew what drove her wild too. Maybe it had to do with knowing each other so well for so long. Or maybe it just came with loving someone and caring about their sexual pleasure more than you did your own.

Whatever it was, sex with Mystic was phenomenal. They'd spent the last few days exploring the new sexual side to their relationship. They not only made love in the guest bedroom, but also in the hayloft, and the labyrinth, and the garden hammock. Although having sex in the hammock had been precarious. Just as things had gotten hot and heavy, the hammock flipped them to the ground.

Thankfully, Stetson and Lily were at the obstetrician's and no one had seen them lying half naked with their clothes tangled around them as they laughed hysterically. But even if they had, Buck doubted anyone would have said a word. He was pretty sure everyone knew what was going on. He had run into Wolfe when he was sneaking back to his room early one morning. Delaney had caught them coming down from the hayloft with hay in their hair. And then there were the family meals when he couldn't keep his eyes off Mystic.

He loved her sitting at the table next to him. She fit into his family like she had always been part of it. And she had. The only difference was that now Mystic seemed to realize it too. She belonged on the ranch.

Buck couldn't be happier.

Or more excited.

She was absolutely going to flip out when she saw the house and her salon.

He squeezed her hand and smiled as they passed the *Welcome to Cursed* sign. Only a few seconds later, the Malone house came into view. It looked almost exactly the same as it had. The shingles on the roof were the same deep brown. The shutters beside each window the same navy blue. Even the same shrubs and flowers had been planted in front of the porch. They weren't as big or full as their predecessors, but they would grow to the same size in a year or so. In the front window hung a fortune-telling and palm reading sign. Kitty had put it there. She had also made sure there were two chairs on the front porch.

It was like the tornado had never happened.

Buck could understand why Mystic and Hester appeared to be stunned speechless when he pulled into the driveway. He'd been stunned too when he'd first seen the house. And thrilled that the town had pulled it off. There were no better people in all of Texas. As he parked, he couldn't help feeling proud as hell to be a member of such a kind, loving town.

He parked and hopped out to open Hester's and Mystic's truck doors. But even when he had Mystic's opened, she just sat there and stared at the house.

"But I don't understand. I thought the house was gone."

"Not anymore." He took her hand and helped her down. "Come on."

As soon as they were headed to the porch, the front door opened and the majority of the townsfolk streamed out, yelling "Surprise!"

Mystic and Hester froze in their tracks and stood there speechless. And anytime anyone was speechless, Kitty Carson was more than happy to fill the silence. She pushed to the front of the group and stood on the top step of the porch, grinning from ear to ear.

"I guess y'all were expecting a hole in the ground. And that was what was here until Buck decided to do a house raisin'."

"Actually, it was Everly's idea," Buck said.

"But you were the one who got the ball rollin'," Kitty continued. "The one who organized everything and made sure the framers, drywallers, electricians, plumbers, carpenters, window installers, door hangers, and carpet layers got the job done right." She looked at Mystic and Hester and grinned her bucktoothed grin. "If we didn't have the right person for the job here in Cursed, Buck found someone who was willing to come here and help. Plus, he fronted the money so we could pay them and didn't have to wait for the insurance money to come through."

"It wasn't that big of a deal," Buck said. "You and the townsfolk were the ones who did all the work." He glanced at Hester and Mystic who were still standing there staring. "I know the Malones appreciate it. I'm sure it's just a little overwhelming."

Hester nodded. "I don't know what to say. Your generosity is more than I ever expected."

"Well, then your expectations are way too low," Kitty said. "Did you think we would let our only fortune-teller leave this town? Hell, no. Your family has been part of this town ever since it started and there's no place else a Malone should be, but right here in Cursed."

Hester's eyes filled with tears. "Well, thank

you." She looked around at the people standing on the porch. "Thank you all. I'm overwhelmed and humbled. Mystic and I can never repay you for your kindness."

"There's no need to repay us," Thelma Davenport said. "You and Mystic are part of our community. We take care of our own."

Tears fell down Hester's cheeks . . . but Mystic's eyes were dry. Obviously, she was still in shock.

Buck took her hand and squeezed it. "You okay, Miss?"

She turned to him. "Why didn't you tell me?"

Kitty didn't let him answer. "Because he wanted to surprise you. That's why he kept you out at the ranch and wouldn't let anyone from town come to see you or Hester. He didn't want you to see a big hole in the ground. He wanted you coming back to your home. There's no need for you to leave Cursed now." She winked at Buck. "Not that Buck would let you. I knew when you and Buck came down to the basement after the tornado that something had changed between you two. Did you see his love aura? Is that how you knew he didn't just love you as a friend?"

He waited to see how Mystic was going to field the question. But she didn't answer Kitty. Instead, she pulled her hand from Buck's and looked at the people standing on the porch.

"Thank you, y'all. Thank you so much. My grandmother is right. There's no way we can ever repay you for this kindness." Her eyes finally welled with tears and she choked out her next words. "I'm—sorry, but I need a second." She turned and hurried around the side of the house.

When she was gone, Kitty shook her head. "Poor thing is just overwhelmed by our generosity. She'll be even more so when she sees her salon."

Buck hoped that was true, but he had a bad feeling in the pit of his stomach. He didn't hesitate to follow Mystic. He found her standing just inside the door of the salon. Everly had done a great job of making the salon look like it had before. With one minor exception: the neon sign that hung on the wall behind the reception desk.

It read *Mystic's* in glowing neon purple.

"What have you done?" Mystic said as she stared at the sign.

"I didn't know Everly was going to rename your salon Mystic's from Cursed Cut and Curl. You can take it down if you don't like it."

She turned to him. "It's not the sign, Buck." She waved a hand around. "It's this entire place. The entire house. Why would you do something like this?"

He felt like she'd slapped him. "What are you talking about?"

"I'm talking about taking it upon yourself to rebuild my home and my business without even consulting me."

He stared at her in confusion. "You didn't want to rebuild?"

She looked at him as if it was a foolish question. "No. I did not. And you knew that. You rebuilt it anyway because you knew that rebuilding the house and my salon would make it almost impossible for me to leave."

His own anger flared. "I didn't plot against you, Missy. I just wanted you to be happy. Staying in Cursed will make you happy. You're just too stubborn to admit it."

"I'm not being stubborn. I'm being logical. Staying in Cursed isn't the right decision for either one of us. You know it and I know it. But you just had to be a Kingman and take charge. You just had to force me to your will. And now when I leave, I'm going to disappoint every single person who worked so hard to finish this house so quickly."

He stared at her. "Leave? You're still planning on leaving?"

Once again tears welled in her eyes, muting the bluish-purple to a soft lavender. "I don't have another choice."

"Yes, you do. You can stay."

She shook her head. "I won't settle for a man who doesn't love me enough."

His temper broke. "Enough? I don't love you enough? I've done everything I can possibly think of to prove my love for you—including completely depleting my entire savings account to build this house and salon—and it's not enough?"

"Material things don't prove love, Buck."

He snorted. "But a fuckin' aura does?"

Her eyes snapped with anger. "I can't help what I can't see."

He grabbed her by the arms and jerked her closer. "Then maybe you should stop looking and start feeling. What do you feel, Missy? Do you love me? Or were those words you spoke this morning just a lie?"

Tears dripped down her cheeks. "Don't do this, Buck."

"Don't do what? Don't try to get to the truth? Don't try to save you from your own screwed-up mind?"

"My mind isn't screwed up. I'm the only one who is thinking clearly."

"If you think that leaving Cursed is thinking clearly, then you are screwed up. You belong here. With me. Deep down, you know it. You're just too scared to take a chance. And I get it. You've had a lot of people leave you and you're terrified I'll leave you too. But leaving me first isn't the answer, Missy. Staying and fighting for what we have is. I love you." He gave her a little shake. "Do you hear me? I'm not going to leave you. Ever."

More tears rolled down her cheeks. "That's the problem," she said in a broken voice. "You won't leave me. Even when you realize that what you feel for me isn't real, you'll stay because you're too damn honorable to break a vow. I can't let you do that. I do love you, Buck. I love you enough to let you go."

He wanted to scream out in frustration. He wanted to scream and shake her until she believed him. But he knew Mystic. The more he pushed, the more she would resist. He could read it in her eyes that she'd already made up her mind and there was nothing he could say or do to change it. And even if he could get her to stay, did he want to spend the rest of his life with a woman who didn't trust his love? Did he want to spend the rest of his life trying to prove they were made for each other?

As much as it hurt, he had to accept that their relationship wasn't going to work. Not because they didn't love each other, but because she couldn't see that love. And she never would.

"You're right." He let his hands drop. "You do need to go. I don't want a woman who sees with her eyes. I want a woman who sees with her heart."

He turned for the door. With each click of his boots on the tile, he prayed she would stop him. She didn't. Pain sliced his heart in two and what was left was only anger. When he reached the door, he spoke without turning around.

"If you leave, don't ever come back, Mystic. Ever. Because what we have will be dead. And there will be no way to resurrect it. Do you understand me? No way in hell."

Chapter Nineteen

There was no describing the pain and anguish that filled Mystic as she watched Buck walk out the salon door. It closed behind him, the tinted glass obscuring his form like a cloud blocking out the sun. Suddenly, she was left in shadow with no hope that the sun's warmth would ever return.

She crumpled down to the couch and covered her face with her hands as wracking sobs came from deep inside her. She didn't know how long she cried before a voice startled her.

"Man, did you fuck that up."

Mystic lifted her head to see Everly leaning in the doorway of the back room.

Mystic wiped the tears from her cheeks. "What are you doing here?"

Everly stepped into the salon. "Listening to the most pathetic conversation I've ever heard in my life."

"You eavesdropped?"

"It's not eavesdropping when I was here first. I was folding towels in the back in preparation for the big reveal, but it sounds like all my efforts—

and all the town's efforts—were for naught." She walked over and handed Mystic the towel she held in her hand. "Here. If you get mascara on that white couch, I'll be thoroughly ticked. That was a pain in the butt to get through the door."

Mystic blotted beneath her eyes. "I didn't ask for anyone to rebuild my salon. If I had known, I would've stopped Buck."

"So I heard. You have big plans to leave town. Even though it looks like that's the last thing you want to do." Everly snorted. "You're a bigger train wreck than I am."

Mystic couldn't deny it. She leaned her head back on the couch and released a long, quivery sigh. "Leaving is the right thing to do. Buck will thank me for it eventually."

Everly laughed. "If you believe that bullshit I have some oceanfront property in Arizona I'd love to sell you. You just ripped that man's heart out. And believe me, I know all about getting your heart ripped out."

Tears dripped down Mystic's cheeks at just the thought of Buck's face when she'd said she was still leaving. She pressed the towel to her eyes and spoke through the terry material. "I just want him to be happy."

"And you don't think you can make him happy?"

She didn't hesitate to answer. "No. No matter how hard I try to become a successful, prominent businesswoman without the taint of the family's psychic powers, I will always be a freakish

Malone. He will always be a Kingman prince. A prince who deserves a princess. Not a witch. The women in my family are destined to be alone."

Everly didn't speak for a long moment and Mystic lifted her head to find her catlike hazel eyes staring at her. They were almost as piercing as Hester's. It turned out she was just as good at reading people. "Ahh, so that's the problem. It's not Buck who can't love you. It's you who can't love yourself."

Mystic's eyes widened. "What?"

"You're placing the blame on Buck for not loving you enough. But the truth is that it has nothing to do with Buck. It's all about you. You can't see how much he loves you because you don't think you're worthy of his love. You're a cursed Malone woman who deserves to be alone."

"No." Mystic shook her head. "That's not it at all. Buck has no love aura."

"It sounds like you don't either. And in order to accept love from other people, we have to love ourselves."

Mystic stared at her. Was Everly right? Had she blocked Buck's aura with her own insecurities and self-doubt? The possibility made even more tears flood her eyes.

The door opened and Kitty Carson stepped in. Mystic brushed her tears away, but she knew there was no way to hide the fact that she'd been crying. Thankfully, as usual, Kitty misread the entire situation.

"I knew the salon would bring you to tears.

And there's much more to see." She held open the door. "Come on, girl. The townsfolk are dying to show you the house."

Mystic wasn't ready to see the house yet. She felt too raw and emotional. It was a relief when Everly intervened.

"Why don't we give Mystic a few minutes alone to deal with this amazing display of y'all's generosity and affection before you show her the house?"

"Of course." Kitty winked at Mystic. "But don't take too long, honey. I've got a special surprise for you that I know is gonna get you sobbing with joy all over again."

"Oh, I'm sure it will," Everly said as she ushered Kitty out the door.

When they were gone, Mystic just sat there feeling stunned and drained. The glowing neon sign on the wall caught her attention. *Mystic's*. Who was Mystic? A successful businesswoman? A love psychic witch? The fortune-teller's granddaughter? Aurora's unwanted daughter?

She realized she didn't know who she was and she never had.

But sitting there crying about it wasn't going to fix it. She had a town to thank.

She got up and headed to the bathroom in the back room to take care of her drippy mascara. Like the salon, the tiny half bath looked exactly like the previous one—right down to the lavender mosaic tile on the floor. There was only one person who had known every detail of the salon. One person she had rambled on and on to about tile and fixtures and shampoo bowls.

She had thought Buck hadn't been listening.

Obviously, she'd been wrong.

He had listened. He'd listened with his heart.

She stared at her reflection in the oval mirror hanging above the sink. A woman stared back at her. A woman with hair too straight and a nose too tipped and a mouth too wide and eyes too much like the Malones'. After the town found out about her gift, she thought she had finally accepted who she was with all her faults. But accepting who you are and loving who you are were two different things. She had accepted who she was, but she still didn't love who she was. She still looked at herself and saw an imperfect freak who wasn't worthy of love.

But the townsfolk didn't agree.

She was standing in a brand-new salon after her other salon had been swept away in a tornado because an entire town of people thought she was worthy of their love. It didn't matter to them that her mother had deserted her or that her grandmother read palms and crystal balls or that she could see auras. They loved her. And yet, here she was hiding away in a bathroom staring in a mirror and finding fault with what she saw.

Buck was right. She *was* screwed up. She had let her mother's—and father's—desertion make her feel unworthy. She had let their faults and hang-ups color the way she saw herself. And the way she saw other people. Instead of focusing on all the love she had, she'd focused on all the love she'd lost. She'd wanted to cling to her unworthiness just like she had clung to the boxes her mother sent. Instead of throwing them away, she'd stacked them in the attic to remind herself of how little she meant to her mother.

But it didn't matter if her mother only thought of her once a year and her father never thought of her at all. It didn't matter because she had an entire town of people who loved her. She had a loving grandmother. And loving friends.

And Buck.

She stared at her reflection in the mirror. "What am I doing?"

"I was just about to ask you the same thing."

She turned to see her grandmother standing there. All her emotions welled to the surface and she stepped into her grandmother's arms. "I'm so sorry, Hessy."

Hester held her close. "No harm. I think the townsfolk know this is all a little overwhelming."

Mystic shook her head. "No, it's not that. I'm sorry for not being more thankful to you for all you've done for me. For giving me a home and loving me. And for putting up with me ignoring my gift and making you feel like your gift was something to be ashamed of."

Hester patted her back. "I understand. It's hard growing up with a woman as talented as I am."

Mystic drew back and laughed. "You are talented. And so am I. Not just as a hairstylist, but also as a psychic. I just can't read myself."

"I told you reading ourselves isn't the Malones' forte."

"I guess I didn't listen." Her smiled faded. "I really messed things up, Hessy. I thought leaving Cursed would fix all my problems, but I just figured out the only way to fix my problems is to fix myself."

"That's usually the case."

"What if I can't? What if my insecurities are too deeply ingrained?"

"Well, then I guess you'll just have to dig. It might take some work to uncover the pain and deal with it, but I know you're up to the task. I didn't raise a wimp."

Mystic smiled. "No, you didn't." She gave her grandmother another hug. "We're staying, Hessy."

"I knew that. You're not a runner like your mama. You're a sticker. Just like me. Now let's go see our new house. The townsfolk are chomping at the bit to show you what they've done."

Mystic messed up her makeup all over again when she saw the time and effort the townsfolk had put into rebuilding the Malone house. Her grandmother, who rarely cried, couldn't keep the tears from her eyes either.

The floor plan was identical to the original, but everything else was brand new. The oakwood floors. The handmade cabinets in the kitchen, bathrooms, and family room. The butcher-block island and quartz countertops in the kitchen. The beautifully tiled backsplashes and showers. The sinks, toilets, and fixtures in the bathroom. Not only had the townsfolk built the house, but they'd also furnished it with items from their own homes. The kitchen cabinets and drawers held mismatched dishes and pots and pans and eating utensils. A small, well-worn table and chairs sat in the nook with a mason jar of fresh flowers in the center.

There was a faded overstuffed couch and chair in the family room along with a bookcase filled with paperback novels—including a few on palm reading and tarot cards. Hester's and Mystic's rooms each had beds covered in soft sheets and homemade quilts that had no doubt been lovingly quilted by someone in the town.

Everly was right. This wasn't a simple gift. This was a monumental display of love.

Mystic was speechless. So it was Hester who spoke with tears glistening in her eyes.

"There are no words to express our gratitude for what y'all have done for us. You have touched our hearts and made us feel blessed to live in a town with such kind and giving folks. We hope one day we will be able to pass that love and kindness on. And once we get settled, everyone is invited to help us celebrate our new home on Halloween." She smiled. "Everyone knows there's no better time for witches to celebrate."

After everyone had a good laugh, people started to take their leave. Mystic and Hester stood on the porch saying their goodbyes. The Kingmans were the last to go. Mystic had a hard time keeping the tears from her eyes as she gave each one a hug. With Buck's absence so obvious, they all must have known something was wrong. Stetson, Wolfe, Gage, and Shane gave her extra-tight hugs while Lily, Gretchen, and Adeline drew back from the hugs with sad smiles. Only Delaney addressed the elephant on the porch.

"What the hell happened? Why did Buck run off like his tail was on fire? It doesn't make sense. Especially when he was the one who organized this house raising and you two have finally figured out you are more than just friends."

"Good Lord, Del." Wolfe rolled his eyes. "You couldn't just keep your mouth shut, could you?"

"Why would I keep my mouth shut when Buck left in a spray of gravel looking like it was the end of the world and Mystic looks like she's about to burst into tears?"

"Maybe because it's none of your business," Stetson said.

"Like hell it isn't. Buck is our brother and Mystic is like our sister." Delaney looked at Mystic. "If there's something we can do to fix it, we need to know."

Mystic's heart squeezed at being considered a Kingman sister. "Thank you. Y'all are like family to me too. But I'm afraid there's nothing you can do. I messed up things pretty badly with Buck and I'm the one who is going to have to fix them." She hesitated. "But first, I need to concentrate on fixing myself."

Delaney opened her mouth to no doubt ask more questions. Before she could, Shane took her hand and pulled her down the porch steps.

"Come on, sugar pea. Let's let Mystic enjoy her new home."

After the Kingmans were gone, Mystic went back inside. She was surprised to find Kitty and

Hester sitting at the table in the kitchen nook enjoying a cup of tea . . . while bickering.

"Don't try and tell me that you don't think Potts is an attractive cowboy, Gossip Girl," Hester said.

"Like I told you before, Witchy Woman. There's nothing going on between me and Ralph." Kitty leaned closer. "Have you seen something you're not telling me about?"

"I've seen the way you two look at each other when you delivered the mail to the Kingman Ranch." Hester's eyes twinkled. "It's almost like you've put a hex on the man."

Kitty's eyes widened. "A hex? I did no such a thing. But if there is a hex for love, I wouldn't mind learning it. A single woman in this town needs all the help she can—" She cut off when she saw Mystic. "There you are! Your grandmother and I were thinking you'd left with the Kingmans." She got up. "And that would've ruined the entire surprise." She glanced back at Hester. "Well, don't just sit there, Witchy Woman. I want you to see this too."

When they got out to the postal truck, Kitty rolled up the back door. "Surprise!" She held out her hands like a game show prize model.

Mystic was struck speechless as she stared at the boxes stacked in the back.

"I know how you feel," Kitty continued. "I about dropped my teeth when all your birthday boxes started showing up at the post office. I mean how in the world did they survive a tornado when nothing else did? But that's life for you.

Just when you think everything has been blown to smithereens, the thing you needed most comes back to you. And I figured you must've loved these birthday presents a lot if you kept them for all these years with everything still inside." She grabbed a box out of the back. "Where do you want me to put them? On the porch like always?"

Mystic stared at the boxes. They weren't all there, but most of them were. They were tattered, but still intact. It was ironic. While she had lost everything else in the tornado, these boxes had come back to her. The things she'd most wanted to lose.

At least, that was what she had tried to convince herself of.

But as she stood there staring at the boxes, the feeling that spread through her body wasn't anger, or frustration, or hate. It was happiness that the birthday boxes had survived and found their way back to her. Maybe she didn't hate them, and the person who sent them, as much as she'd thought. Which was why she had kept the boxes. Maybe, deep down, she was glad her mother hadn't forgotten her. The boxes were the one connection she had to Aurora.

She grabbed a box out of the back of the postal truck. "Let's put them in my room."

Once the boxes were stacked in the corner of her room and Kitty had left, she and her grandmother stood looking at the boxes.

"The fates have a dark sense of humor," Hester said.

Mystic laughed. "They do, don't they?"

"Shall we have a bonfire? I heard the temperature is going to drop tonight."

"No," Mystic said. "I think I'll open them. I'm sure there are things we can use."

Hester nodded. "Then I'll leave you to it and go make us something to eat. The refrigerator is filled with more casseroles than we'll be able to eat in a year. I guess this town isn't as narrow minded as I thought." She hesitated and turned back to Mystic. "I know I haven't worked very hard to fit in. I'm sorry for that. I know it's made things hard for you."

Mystic couldn't deny it, but she'd made her own mistakes. "And I worked much too hard to fit in. I think we've both learned some lessons, Hessy. I need to embrace the Malones' uniqueness."

"And I need to do more than just read palms and tell fortunes. I need to start living life." Hester's eyes narrowed. "Maybe I'll get myself a hot cowboy too."

Once she was gone, Mystic started opening the boxes . . . and the cards. There were only two words written at the bottom of every card. *Love, Mom.* At one time, those words had seemed like the worst hypocrisy. But now, Mystic saw them differently. Aurora was exactly like Mystic. She had let her father's desertion make her feel like she wasn't worthy of love. So she pushed it away . . . and was still pushing it away.

Mystic could be like her mother and run from love. She could wander the country and avoid heartache by having no connection with anyone. Or she could stay in Cursed and embrace all the joy and pain that came with being part of a community—part of a family.

The choice was hers.

Chapter Twenty

"You're up early."

Buck finished dismounting Mutt and turned to the shadowed man standing in the open doorway of the stables. At first, he thought it was Stetson. The build was right. So was the deep timbre of his voice. But when the man stepped out into the sunlight, Buck realized his mistake.

"Good mornin', Hayden."

"Good mornin'. Looks like you two had a hard ride." Hayden took the reins from Buck. Because of his rodeo experience, Buck had put him to work in the stables with Tab. It had been a good choice. Hayden seemed to have a connection with horses that few people had. Even now, his attention was solely on Mutt. After he swept his hand along the horse's sweaty neck, his gaze returned to Buck. It was easy to read his accusation.

"You're right," Buck said. "I shouldn't have ridden him so hard."

Hayden nodded. "He's an intuitive horse. It looks like he knew you needed a hard ride so he gave you his all."

Buck *had* needed a hard ride, but he shouldn't have taken his frustrations out on a horse. He held out his hand. "I'll cool him down. It's only right." After Hayden handed him the reins, he walked Mutt into the stables and removed his saddle.

"You want to talk about it?"

He glanced over Mutt's back to see Hayden standing in the doorway. "Not really." He didn't want to talk about Mystic. Or think about her. Unfortunately, she was all he could think about. Which explained his lack of sleep and surly disposition.

"Well, keeping it in sure doesn't look like it's working." Hayden said as he unrolled the hose.

He had a good point.

When Buck finished removing the saddle and blanket, he spoke. "She claims she loves me. But if you love someone—really love them—you don't just let them go without a word. It's been close to a week and she hasn't called or even texted. That's not love."

Hayden turned on the hose and started to rinse off Mutt. "Have you tried to contact her?"

"She broke it off with me. Why would I try to contact her?"

Hayden shrugged. "Maybe because you're going crazy without her."

"I was going crazy with her. What kind of woman doesn't believe you when you tell her you love her? And not only that, I worked my ass off making her salon perfect and she didn't even say thank you. Instead, she got all pissed off because she thought it was all a conspiracy I cooked up to get her to stay."

"And was it?"

"Hell no."

Hayden studied him. Even the way he narrowed his eyes reminded Buck of Stetson. "You sure about that? If it wasn't, then why did you keep it a secret?"

"Because I know how stubborn Mystic can be. She would've fought me on it. And she doesn't know what's good for her. She would never be happy living anywhere but Cursed. She's just too stubborn to see it."

"But that wasn't your call. It's Mystic's call on where she wants to live—whether it makes her happy or not. Or whether it makes you happy. By rebuilding her salon, it sounds like you forced her hand. I would've been pissed too. Nobody likes to be shoved in a corner."

"I didn't shove her in the corner." But even as he said the words, he knew it was a lie. Whether it was conscious or subconscious, he had taken her choice away. She couldn't leave Cursed now. Not after the town had worked so hard rebuilding her house and business.

He sighed. "If I had given her a choice, she would've left."

Hayden nodded. "But she might've come back too. And maybe that's all she wants now—time to make her own choice."

Buck's temper flared again. "How much time? A month? A year? Five years?" He shook his head. "I'm not going to wait that long for Mystic to make up her mind that I love her enough."

Hayden turned off the hose and rolled it up. "According to the gossip I've heard, it took you a good long while to figure out Mystic was the woman you wanted."

"That's not true. Deep down, I always knew she was the one for me. I was just too . . ." He struggled to find the right word. Hayden supplied it.

"Chickenshit?"

Buck searched for a better word choice, but realized there wasn't one. He *had* been too chickenshit to tell Mystic how he felt. He'd been terrified she only loved him as a friend and he'd look like a fool. And being a fool scared the hell out of him. Which was why he had refused to take on the responsibility of becoming a boss. He'd been scared he couldn't meet his family's, or the town's, expectations of what a Kingman should be. So he'd sat back and refused to take any responsibility at all.

"You're right," he said. "I am a chickenshit."

Hayden held up a hand. "I didn't call you a chickenshit. I just said you were too chickenshit to state your mind. And we've all been there. Sometimes it's not easy to face the truth head on. But it sounds like Mystic gave you plenty of time to figure out what you wanted. Maybe you should do the same for her." He took Mutt's reins and led him toward his stall.

On the way back to the house, Buck thought about everything Hayden had said. Rebuilding Mystic's business hadn't been Buck's place. He had been hoping it would keep her in Cursed. If he was honest, he still hoped it would. But that wasn't his decision. It was Mystic's. He couldn't force her to stay. Just like he couldn't force her to trust his love.

Which left only one question?

Was he willing to wait for her to figure things out? Or was he going to throw in the towel and quit? She already thought he didn't love her enough. Quitting on her would certainly prove the point. Love shouldn't have a timeline. It should be forever.

But waiting was hell.

For the next few days, he kept his phone with him constantly, hoping Mystic would call. And at least once a day, he made some excuse for going into town in hopes he'd run into her. But he didn't see her once in Cursed. According to Kitty, Mystic was "busy as a spring bee" putting the finishing touches on the house and working in her salon. Buck felt both happy and annoyed. He was glad she was settling in as if she planned to stay and annoyed she didn't seem to be missing him at all.

Maybe he'd been wrong.

Maybe she didn't love him after all.

Then one morning, when he was getting out of the shower, his cellphone pinged with an incoming text. He ignored it while he got dressed. As he headed down to breakfast, he picked up his phone and glanced at the screen.

The words in the text bubble had him coming to a sudden halt. It was a reminder of his hair appointment tomorrow morning at nine o'clock. It wasn't from Mystic's cellphone. It was from Mystic's salon. Was it a fluke? Had Mystic recovered her scheduling program and the program had automatically sent the reminder?

But tomorrow wasn't the first Wednesday of the month. It wasn't even a Wednesday. It was Monday. And Mystic didn't work on Mondays.

His thumb hovered over the message keyboard for only a second before he hit *C* for confirm.

The next twenty-four hours, he was nothing but a jumble of nerves. That morning, he nicked himself twice while shaving, changed shirts five times, and hats twice. By the time he finally pulled into the lot next to the Malone's house, he was late by a good thirty minutes. At the door of the salon, he wiped his sweaty palms on his jeans before he pulled open the door and stepped inside.

No one was there. It looked like the text *was* a fluke. With a sad sinking feeling in the pit of his stomach, he turned to leave. But before he could push open the door, Mystic spoke.

"Goin' somewhere, Buckaroo?"

He turned to find her standing in the doorway of the back room. His breath stalled in his lungs as he took in all the colors of Mystic.

She wore the turquoise cowboy boots he'd bought her for Christmas and the bright floral dress that hugged her breasts and petite waist and showed off her legs. She'd fixed her jet-black hair into a mass of curls that framed the delicate features of her face and painted her bowed lips his favorite color of red.

Her soft lavender eyes pierced straight through his soul. In those eyes, he read something that made his heart trip faster. But he was too gun shy to make the first move. So he just stood there until she finally broke their silent stare-down.

"You're late." She moved into the salon with a confidence he hadn't seen before. "And where's my coffee?"

"Sorry, I wasn't sure if I had an appointment."

She opened the top drawer at her station and pulled out a plastic cape. "I figured you would need a trim so I switched our standing date."

"Date?"

Her eyes softened . . . as did her voice. "That's what it was for me. A date where I got to let down my guard and touch you like I longed to touch you the rest of the month."

He stepped closer, his heart pounding in his ears. "You could've touched me anytime you wanted to, Missy."

She shook her head. "I wasn't ready." She smiled. "But I think I am now."

He wanted to touch her too. He wanted to pull her into his arms and kiss her until she was as breathless as he was. But he didn't want to force things. He wanted her to set the pace. So he sat down in the chair like he always did and waited for her to spread the cape around his shoulders. As she snapped it, her fingers brushed his neck and a tremble ran through his body.

Their gazes caught in the mirror. "Your hair has

gotten long," she said in a voice that was husky and sexy as hell. She slid her fingers through his hair, sending tingling heat along his scalp. "But I like it. Maybe I should just give you a shampoo. What do you think?"

He had to swallow down the thick swell of desire that had risen to his throat. "Do whatever you want, Miss."

Again, their gazes caught in the mirror. "I think I like my Buckaroo with long hair. Now come on, let's get you shampooed."

Mystic's shampoos had always relaxed him. Not today. Today, his head felt like one of those plasma balls and Mystic's fingers were sending bolts of desire arcing through him. It didn't help that her breasts were inches from his mouth. Breasts he had cradled and kissed and suckled . . . and wanted to cradle, kiss, and suckle again.

He slammed his eyes closed and tried to relax. But the more she massaged his scalp, the hotter he became. It was a relief when she started rinsing. He waited until she had dried his hair before he opened his eyes. She was standing over him, still holding the towel, with a look in her violet eyes that took his breath away.

As he watched, she lowered her head. The kiss was soft and sweet and the best kiss he'd ever received in his life.

She drew back and smiled. "You don't know how many times I wanted to do that."

"How many?"

"Over the years? Hundreds."

He sat up. "Why didn't you?"

She folded the towel over the edge of the sink. "Because I was confused about what love was. I thought it was something you had to get before you gave. I didn't realize that it's the other way around. It's something you have to give before you can fully receive." She looked at him with tears in her eyes. "I was scared to fully give you my love, Buck. Scared you'd hurt me like my mama did."

He took her hand. "I would never hurt you, Missy. I *will* never hurt you."

She smiled sadly. "Yes, you will. Love hurts sometimes and that's just part of caring for someone. I care for my mama and it hurts. I can't pretend like it doesn't. But I don't have to let that hurt make me run from love. And that's what I was doing with you, Buck. Running from love. It was safer for me to ignore all the evidence of your love, just like I did with Mama's boxes, than it was to accept the wonderful gift you offered me."

"And now you can accept that I love you?" He lifted his brows. "Even without an aura?"

Tears welled in her eyes as she nodded. "I don't want to be a woman who sees with her eyes. I want to be a woman who feels with her heart. I've felt your love ever since we were kids. You're my North Star—the one constant I can count on."

His hand tightened on hers, and Buck didn't even try to hold back the tears that flooded his eyes. "And you're mine, Miss. Wherever you lead, I'll follow.

Her smile was wobbly. "Liar. You'll never follow me into a carnival funhouse."

"No person in their right mind should go into those nightmares. But I'll follow you any place besides a spooky carnival funhouse."

She laughed, but then quickly sobered. "What about Holy Gospel this Saturday?"

He looked at her with confusion. "Why? They don't have church services on Saturday."

"It's not a church service. It's a wedding."

Hope welled in his heart. "And just who's getting married?"

Her smile was soft and hesitant. "Two childhood friends who realized they want to spend forever together and want that forever to start as soon as possible."

It was hard to speak over the pounding of his heart. "Are you asking me to marry you, Mystic Malone?"

"I'm asking you to marry me, Buck Kingman. If you're not ready, I understand. I hurt you and I'm sorry—"

He pulled her onto his lap and kissed her like he had wanted to kiss her since she'd stepped out of the back room. When he finally drew back, he smiled and gave her an answer. An answer he'd had ready for a lifetime. "Yes. I'll marry you, Mystic Twilight Malone. But you do realize that this Saturday is Halloween."

She smiled wickedly. "What better day for a witch to jump over the broom."

Chapter Twenty-One

"I WISH I HAD SEEN THIS day. It certainly would've made my life less stressful." Hester moved up behind Mystic. As usual, Hester was dressed in solid black—regardless of the fact that this was her granddaughter's wedding day.

Of course, Mystic wasn't dressed like most brides on their wedding day either. The dress she'd chosen was short and a soft lavender. Her bridal shoes were cowboy boots that matched. She had no veil. Although she had purchased a cute little purple witch's hat fascinator to wear for the reception at Nasty Jack's.

As she looked at her and her grandmother's reflections in the full-length mirror, Mystic accepted the fact that they might not be the fairest in all the land, but they were definitely the most unique. The Malone women never did anything like everyone else.

She smiled at Hester. "I thought you said that sometimes it's best if we don't see what life has in store for us."

"True." Tears filled Hester's eyes. "This moment

wouldn't be as special if I'd seen what a beautiful bride you'd make."

"Oh, Hessy." Mystic turned and pulled her grandmother into her arms. "I love you."

Hester squeezed her tightly. "I love you too, Mystic Twilight. More than you will ever know."

The guilt Mystic had been dealing with the last few days reared its ugly head. She'd spent the last night she'd spend under the same roof as her grandmother. All her things had already been packed and moved to Buck's room at the Kingman Ranch. Even though Mystic would still work at the salon and see Hester every single day, she couldn't stand the thought of Hester eating breakfast and dinner all by herself. Or going up to her room every night with no one to say good night to. Buck knew how Mystic felt and had offered to move into town. But Hester would have none of it.

Still, Mystic kept trying.

"Are you sure you don't want me and Buck to move in here, Hessy?"

Hester drew back and sent her a stern look. "I'll hear no more of that. Buck's a rancher, and ranchers need to live on a ranch."

"But it's not that far to the Kingman Ranch. Buck would be just as happy living here as he would be living there."

Hester patted her cheek. "As long as he's with you, I know Buck will be happy. But did you ever think that maybe I wouldn't be happy with a man living in this house. Men can mess up psychic energy like nobody's business. I couldn't see a thing when your granddaddy was living here."

Mystic laughed. "Buck does seem to screw up my psychic power." She still couldn't read his aura. But since learning to love herself, Mystic's psychic sight with other people had grown. Everywhere she went, she saw golden auras. Something she planned to keep to herself. She had accepted her powers, but she had also learned that love wasn't something you should stick your nose into.

"Well, I can't take the chance that Buck will mess up my sight," Hester said. "Now stop fretting. I'm looking forward to having the house all to myself. I read an article on a psychic website about how reading your crystal ball completely naked can increase the energy flow and I want to try it out."

The thought of her grandmother running around the house naked was an image Mystic could do without. It was a relief when the doorbell rang and she could end the conversation.

"I'll get it."

"You can't get it. What if it's Buck? It's bad luck for the groom to see the bride on the day of the wedding."

It was too late for that. Buck had snuck in her room last night and hadn't left until early that morning. She'd woken up to him smiling down at her and whispering, "Happy Wedding Day, my love."

She had no doubt it would be.

"It's not Buck," she said. "It's probably my maid of honor and bridesmaids." She had told Delaney she didn't need any help getting ready and would just meet her, Adeline, Gretchen, and Lily at the church. She knew Delaney didn't mind skipping all the female fussing. But Mystic figured the other Kingman women didn't feel the same way and wanted to be part of the bridal preparation.

Not that Mystic needed any help. She was running way ahead of schedule and was completely ready. Which was strange for a woman who liked everything to be timed exactly. Or maybe not so strange considering that she'd been waiting all her life to head down the aisle to Buck. The sooner the better.

But when Mystic opened the front door, it wasn't her new sisters-in-law standing there. It was a woman with hair as black as Mystic's and eyes just as violet.

Mystic was more than a little stunned. She had invited her mama to the wedding, but she hadn't thought Aurora would show up. She hadn't even been sure her mama would still be living at the address Stetson's investigator had found. And yet, here she was. Now Mystic worried she'd made a big mistake. What if Aurora's presence ruined her special day like it had ruined her birthdays?

But as she looked at her mother, she didn't feel angry. Or resentful. Or inadequate. All she felt was sympathy for a woman who had been too scared to embrace love.

Mystic wasn't scared anymore.

She held open her arms. "Mama!"

Buck was scared.

Mystic was late. And she was never late.

As he stood at the front of the church waiting for his bride to walk down the aisle, his heart felt like a squirrel trying to get out of a trap.

He shot a glance over at the maid of honor.

Instead of easing his obvious panic in a soft whisper, Delaney spoke loud enough for people in the next county to hear. "Don't look at me? I don't know what's keeping your bride."

Wolfe rested a hand on his shoulder and leaned close to whisper, "She'll be here."

But Buck wasn't as sure. He shouldn't have let her rush the wedding. He knew she had only done it for him because he'd always been in such a hurry to get married. But he wasn't in a hurry now. He didn't need marriage. Or even kids. All he needed was Mystic. When she finally appeared at the back of the church with Hester and a dark-haired, violet-eyed woman who could only be a Malone, he knew what had kept her.

Her mama had shown up.

As happy as he was for Mystic, her late arrival had made him realize that he didn't want her doing this just to please him. He waited for Hester to walk her down the aisle. When Mystic reached him, he took her hands in his. "We don't have to do this if you're not ready."

She looked taken back. "What happened to the man who couldn't wait to get married?"

"He realized that marriage is more than just a word. It's a pact made between two people to be the best of friends forever." He smiled. "As I remember it, we already made that pact, Missy. I can wait as long as you need to make it legal."

She blinked back the tears that filled her eyes. "I love you, Buck. You *are* my best friend. Forever. Now quit stalling, because I can't wait a second longer to become your legal wife."

Joy filled him and he couldn't help but sweep her up in his arms and kiss her. The townsfolk cheered. Once the cheers had died down, Chance cleared his throat to start the ceremony. But Buck and Mystic paid no attention and kept right on kissing.

"Give it up, Preach," Everly yelled out. "Just get to the 'I dos' and pronounce them man and wife so we can get to the drinking."

After a sigh of exasperation, that's exactly what Chance did.

The town *did* get to drinking. Someone spiked the punch with tequila. By the time the toasts were made and the cake was cut and the garter and bouquet were tossed, there wasn't a sober person at the reception. Even the town preacher got a little tipsy and started dancing.

"I'm glad Chance is having fun," Mystic said as Buck whirled her around the dance floor. "If any man needs some joy in his life, Chance does. It's so sad about his wife."

Buck agreed. He wouldn't know what to do without his Missy. He pulled her closer and kissed her. "Are you ready to call it a night, Mrs. Kingman? I've had a major hard-on since removing your garter and getting a peek of your panties."

She swatted him. "Buck Kingman!"

He grinned. "Hey, old habits are hard to break. I don't know how many times I've tried to get a peek at your panties over the years. I even stole a pair out of your dresser drawer when we were thirteen."

Mystic tried to look appalled, but the twinkle in her violet eyes and the smile tugging at her lips said otherwise. "Why, you little thief. And just what did you do with those panties?"

He grinned sheepishly. "You really don't want to know."

Mystic laughed. "You're probably right."

He waltzed her around the dance floor a couple more times before he leaned close and whispered in her ear, "Missy?"

"Hmm?"

"Can we head home so I can steal your panties again?"

She drew back, her eyes soft with love. "Yes, Buckaroo. Let's go home."

Outside, his green monster truck was parked right up front and decorated with a *Just Married* sign and a string of paper hearts that it looked like everyone in town had written well wishes on.

He opened the passenger side door for Mystic, but she didn't get in. Instead, she held out her hand. "Hand over your keys. You've had too much to drink."

"Now wait a second, Missy, you were drinking tonight too. Maybe not the punch, but you had champagne."

"That wasn't champagne. That was ginger ale. Now give me your keys."

He pulled the keys out of his pocket, but then hesitated. "Are you sure you can handle Frog?"

She lifted her eyebrows. He gave her the keys.

She handled the big ol' truck surprisingly well for a little bit of a thing. She looked sexy as hell doing it. Her short wedding dress rode high on her thighs and hugged her curves in all the right places. She had a cute little witch's hat perched on her dark curls.

Buck smiled. Who needs a princess when they could have a sexy witch? A witch who had thoroughly cast a spell on him. He wished the truck had a bench seat so he could snuggle next to his witch.

A thought struck him. "I think I just figured out what to get you as a wedding present. How would you like an old pickup with a bench seat?"

"No, thank you."

"Then what do you want? And don't say you have everything you need. I'm buying you a wedding gift, Miss."

She waited to answer until she had pulled up in front of Buckinghorse Palace. A big ol' harvest moon hung over the turrets of the castle and shone in Mystic's eyes when she turned to him. "How about a blue SUV with plenty of room in the back so none of our children have to ever ride in another car?"

He laughed, thinking she was making a joke about their game of Life. But his laughter died when Mystic didn't join in. He glanced down at her hand resting on her stomach and his eyes widened.

"Missy?"

She smiled softly. "I'm not positive. But I'm late and I just have this feeling."

If Buck trusted anyone's feelings, he trusted Mystic's. He hopped out of the truck and hurried around to pull her out of her seat and hold her close. "How? When?"

She laughed. "I think you know how, Buck Kingman. As for when, it happened when I was staying at the ranch. Probably that day in the hayloft when you didn't have a condom, but swore you pulled out in time."

The hayloft. It seemed appropriate since that was where he'd first realized how much he loved Mystic.

"A baby," he whispered as he drew back and reverently placed a hand on her stomach. "Maybe even two." A big grin spread over his face.

Mystic shook her head. "Oh, no, I will not have a child named Tater."

Instead of answering, Buck kissed her.

He wasn't worried about what they'd name their kids . . . he'd always been able to talk Mystic into anything.

THE END

Turn the page for a special SNEAK PEEK of the next Kingman Ranch novel!

SNEAK PEEK!
Charming a Christmas Texan
coming December 2022!

WEDDING RECEPTIONS WERE THE PERFECT setting for bad choices.

Not that Everly Grayson had ever made good ones. Her choices in life had always leaned toward the bad. Which is how she ended up quitting high school and running away to Dallas to become a tattoo artist. Falling head over heels in love with her best friend. And managing a bar in a Podunk Texas town when she hated small towns with a passion.

But last night at Buck and Mystic Kingman's wedding reception, she had taken her bad decision-making one step further.

Everly stared at the man lying in the bed next to her. His features were identical to his twin brother's. But she had always been able to tell the two apart. Mostly because Chance Ransom scowled whenever she was around.

He wasn't scowling now. His face was relaxed in sleep, his lips slightly parted and emitting a huff of air on each exhalation. His sandy locks were usually styled back from his face with not a hair out of place. This morning, the thick strands shot up in spiky tufts that softened his stern features and gave him a boyish look. Although there was nothing boyish about the dark stubble that covered his strong jaw.

Everly had always loved a little stubble. She liked the way it looked and she liked the way it felt against her skin when a man's face was right between her—

Hell, no, Everly James Grayson. Don't you even think it. You already made a big mistake. You don't need to compound it.

She reached over and shook Chance awake. "Time to rise and shine."

Chance's long lashes slowly opened. His eyes crinkled at the corners in confusion as he glanced around. Either the sudden movement or the early morning sun coming in the window caused him to cringe and slam his eyes shut again. She figured he had one helluva of a hangover. Her head pounded and she hadn't downed half as much wedding punch as Chance had.

What the hell had been in that punch?

Chance massaged his temples and groaned. "Good Lord."

"I don't know if the Lord had anything to do with last night," she said.

With a jerk of his head, Chance turned to her. She'd thought his eyes were the same soft brown as Shane's. But this close, she realized that there was nothing soft about Chance's eyes. The pupils were hard onyx surrounded by a ring of deep coffee. They held surprise for a split second and then horror. Like she was the worse possible nightmare he'd ever had.

She figured to a pastor, she was.

She grinned. "Good mornin', Preach."

He continued to stare at her. "What are you doing in my bed?"

She stretched her arms over her head and yawned loudly. "I think that should be my question, Goldilocks."

He sat straight up, cringing from the pain that no doubt ricocheted through his head. He looked around the room and then back at her before he covered his face with both his hands and muttered. "What have I done?"

She was feeling the same way. But she had never been someone who spent a lot of time on regret.

"Now, Preach," she said. "It's not a big deal. All people sin from time to time. Even holier-than-thou preachers. I'm sure God will forgive you for one night of debauchery."

He lowered his hands and stared at her. "Debauchery?"

"Well, maybe not debauchery as much as a little wicked fun. And there's nothing wrong with a little wicked fun." Everly reached out and patted his forearm.

It was hard not to notice the flex of muscles beneath her palm . . . or the ones stacked up his stomach to his chest. Chance's body had surprised her. She'd thought a preacher would be pale from lack of sun and puny from lack of exercise. But she'd been way off base. A caramel tan covered defined pectorals, biceps, and two rows of tummy muscles. Shane had a nice body, but if Everly was honest—and she was always honest—Chance's wasn't just nice. It was . . . lickable.

Not that she had licked it. Or that she would ever lick it. But last night, eating him like a chocolate mocha ice cream cone had crossed her mind.

Okay, maybe it was still crossing her mind.

Chance uttered a very unpreacher-like curse beneath his breath and jumped out of bed.

Or tried to.

The sheet caught around his feet and he almost took a header to the floor. He kicked free and stood. She tried to look away—okay, maybe she didn't try that hard. Speaking of hard. She got a glimpse of a great ass and an impressive morning erection before he grabbed the sheet and wrapped it around his waist.

He stared at her. "Tell me what happened."

She fluffed the pillows and reclined back, uncaring of where the sheet settled. Chance's gaze lowered for a brief second before it quickly lifted. The annoyance in his eyes was easy to read. He, either, didn't like the shorty tank top she slept in or her belly button ring. Whatever it was, she refused to let his censorship make her feel inferior.

"You should've seen the piercing I had in my nose. I hated to get rid of it, but it kept getting caked with boogers."

His annoyed look grew. "Do you have to share everything?"

She shrugged. "I thought the Bible says 'The truth will set you free.'"

"Jesus wasn't talking about telling everyone your personal information. He was talking about the truth of the Word of God. If you know God's truth, it will set you free."

She studied him. "Hmm? You know God's word and you don't seem very free. In fact, you seem as tense as a clock that has been wound too tightly and needs to be sprung in order to keep ticking." She laughed. "And it looks like all you needed was a little spiked punch to get sprung."

"It's not funny." He ran a hand through his hair and looked around as if searching for help. "What happened last night was wrong. All wrong. I shouldn't have even attended the reception. I shouldn't have accepted the cup of punch. Or any of the ones after. And I certainly shouldn't have gone to bed . . . " He glanced back at her. "With you."

The entire scenario of a Ransom twin telling her what a mistake he'd made by sleeping with her was like déjà vu. Suddenly, she wasn't having fun anymore prodding the preacher. She decided to let him off the hook.

"Well, you certainly aren't my first choice either, Preach. So I guess we're both lucky that nothing happened last night."

He stared at her suspiciously. "Then why am I naked?"

"Because you stripped off all your clothes before you passed out in my bed. I found you after I closed up the bar."

"And you joined me instead of trying to wake me up?"

"I was a little tipsy myself. Not to mention, exhausted from pouring drinks all night for the entire town. Walking down the hall to the other room seemed like too much effort. Besides, it's my bed. You were the interloper. And what did you want me to do? Send you home falling down drunk? If I had let the new preacher get run over or stumble and crack open your head, the town would tar and feather me. If word gets out that you spent the night in the Evil Everly Grayson's bed, they still might."

He stared at her. In his eyes, she saw the strong need to believe her. Finally, his shoulders relaxed and he released his breath. "Thank God." Holding the sheet, he picked up his clothing scattered over the floor and walked out of the room. A few seconds later, she heard the bathroom door slam.

She blew out her breath and rubbed her aching temples. "Way to go, Everly. You just couldn't learn your lesson the first time, could you?"

The toilet flushed, making her realize how badly she had to go. She got up and searched for her jeans. Once she pulled them on, she headed downstairs.

Nasty Jack's was a typical small town Texas honky-tonk. It had a well-worn pool table, a boot-heel-scarred dance floor, an old .45 jukebox, a bunch of mismatched tables and chairs, and a long bar that covered one entire wall. Christmas lights hung year-round above the bar and classic beer signs glowed from the walls.

The only thing that made Nasty Jack's different from most small town bars was the pie. The owner's wife made them from scratch. Gretchen Kingman knew how to bake a pie. The short time Everly had managed the bar, she had become addicted to the tasty treat. There was something about the flaky crust and gooey fillings that made her feel better about her bad life choices.

After using the women's bathroom, she headed to the kitchen in search of some pie comfort. She found half of a raspberry peach pie hidden beneath a dishtowel. After making a strong pot of coffee—another addiction—she poured herself a mug full, grabbed a fork, and sat down at the prep island to indulge.

As she ate, she heard the sound of cowboy boots clicking against the hardwood floor. She figured Chance would sneak out the door without a word. She was surprised when the clicking grew closer and he walked in through the swinging door.

Damn, she loved a man in a Stetson. The brown felt of his hat matched his eyes. But the rest of him looked pretty pathetic. His dress shirt and pants were wrinkled. His eyes were red-rimmed and the skin under his dark stubble grayish. When he removed his hat, his hair looked like he'd tried to smooth it down . . . without success.

He stood there holding his hat like a guilty schoolboy. "I owe you an apology, Everly. I shouldn't have assumed you were responsible for me being in your bed."

She took the bite of pie and shrugged. "No sweat, Preach. I've had worse assumptions made about me."

"Well, I was wrong. And I'd appreciate it if you didn't . . ." He let the sentence drift off, but she knew what he was asking.

She mimed zipping her lips. "My lips are sealed as tight as Tupperware. Although you're still going to be the subject of gossip. I don't think the town realized how well their new preacher danced."

He stared at her. "I danced?"

"A lot. You even dipped Miss Kitty."

Chance rubbed his temples and groaned. "I'm sure the church board is already planning a meeting to fire me."

"Doubtful. If they didn't fire you for punching a Kingman—and we all know how much they worship the Kingmans—I doubt they'll fire you for doing a little drinking and dancing at a wedding. Especially when everyone was drinking and dancing and having the time of their lives."

Chance lowered his hand and studied her. "Except for you. If I remember correctly, you didn't appear to be having the time of your life."

"I was bartending."

"And watching Shane."

Even drunk, the preacher was observant. She shrugged. "What can I say? Shane is a good dancer. Did you two take lessons when you were kids?"

He didn't fall for the subject change. "Give it up, Everly. Shane is happy."

The pie in her stomach threatened to come back up. She dropped the fork into the metal pie plate and took a sip of coffee before she spoke. "I know your brother is happy."

"Do you?" He stepped closer. "Then why did you take the job here in Cursed? With your business degree and experience managing restaurants, you could have easily found a managerial position anywhere. Why here?"

"Wolfe and Gretchen Kingman needed help. What can I say? I'm a giving person."

Chance shook his head. "That wasn't the reason. The real reason is that you're still not over my brother, and you think if you hang out long enough in Cursed, Shane will realize what a mistake he made marrying Delaney and come running back to you."

She snorted. "Wow, you have some imagination, Preach. I'm not still pining for Shane."

"Really? What color shirt did he have on last night?"

As much as she didn't want to know, she did. Green and yellow plaid with a touch of baby blue. She got up on shaky legs that didn't feel like they could support her. But Everly had always been good at beating the odds.

Except for love.

Those odds had beaten her soundly.

But she refused to let Chance know it.

She smiled. "Sorry to cut you off, Preach, but I've got better things to do on my day off than listen to a sermon from the town pastor. If I want to get preached at, I'll come to your church."

She went to sweep past him, but his hand shot out and grabbed her arm. His dark eyes glittered with warning. "Shane is never going to leave

Delaney for you, Everly. I'll make sure of it. So go home to Dallas. There's nothing for you in Cursed."

© Charming a Christmas Texan excerpt by Katie Lane

Preorder Today!
https://tinyurl.com/5awnydhs

Other Titles by Katie Lane

Be sure to check out all of Katie Lane's novels!
www.katielanebooks.com

Kingman Ranch Series:
Charming a Texas Beast
Charming a Knight in Cowboy Boots
Charming a Big Bad Texan
Charming a Fairytale Cowboy
Charming a Texas Prince
Charming a Christmas Texan (December 2022)

Bad Boy Ranch Series:
Taming a Texas Bad Boy
Taming a Texas Rebel
Taming a Texas Charmer
Taming a Texas Heartbreaker
Taming a Texas Devil
Taming a Texas Rascal
Taming a Texas Tease
Taming a Texas Christmas Cowboy

Brides of Bliss Texas Series:
Spring Texas Bride
Summer Texas Bride
Autumn Texas Bride
Christmas Texas Bride

Tender Heart Texas Series:
Falling for Tender Heart
Falling Head Over Boots
Falling for a Texas Hellion
Falling for a Cowboy's Smile
Falling for a Christmas Cowboy

Deep in the Heart of Texas Series:
Going Cowboy Crazy
Make Mine a Bad Boy
Catch Me a Cowboy
Trouble in Texas
Flirting with Texas
A Match Made in Texas
The Last Cowboy in Texas
My Big Fat Texas Wedding

Overnight Billionaires Series:
A Billionaire Between the Sheets
A Billionaire After Dark
Waking up with a Billionaire

Hunk for the Holidays Series:
Hunk for the Holidays
Ring in the Holidays
Unwrapped

About the Author

KATIE LANE IS A FIRM believer that love conquers all and laughter is the best medicine. Which is why you'll find plenty of humor and happily-ever-afters in her contemporary and western contemporary romance novels. A USA Today Bestselling Author, she has written numerous series, including *Deep in the Heart of Texas, Hunk for the Holidays, Overnight Billionaires, Tender Heart Texas, The Brides of Bliss Texas, Bad Boy Ranch,* and *Kingman Ranch*. Katie lives in Albuquerque, New Mexico, and when she's not writing, she enjoys reading, eating chocolate (dark, please), and snuggling with her high school sweetheart and Cairn Terrier, Roo.

For more on her writing life or just to chat, check out Katie here:
Facebook *www.facebook.com/katielaneauthor*
Instagram *www.instagram.com/katielanebooks*

And for information on upcoming releases and great giveaways, be sure to sign up for her mailing list at *www.katielanebooks.com*!